THE MEANEST DOLL IN THE WORLD

DOLL HOUSES

26117. Solid wood. One the most popular design Brick details. Façade open door. Price.....

26118. High quality. Front-opening doll house with brass hinges. Two chimneys. Eight rooms. Heart-shaped lock keeps dolls securely inside.

Price.....$13.00

26119. Shingled doll house with enclosed porch. Price.....$15.00

AUNT DOLLS

6120. Brilliantly decorated hat with pink bows. The costume is a work of art, made of the finest silk with lace trim. Ivory buttons. With bisque head and limbs, and painted hair. Price.$2.00

26121. Same: with violet coat and flowing hair......$2.75

DOLL FURNITURE

26122. Made of hardwood with handsome carved back. This chair comes with oak table with turned legs. Price.....$1.00

KITCHEN SUPPLIES

26126. Tin kitchen set. Small size. Price.....$0.20

UNCLE DOLLS

26123. Bisque head. Tweed suit. Price.....$1.50

26124. Same as above with shiny gold watch chain. Price.....$1.75

26125. Same as above with striped suit and silk top hat. Price.....$1.85

DOLL SUNDRIES

26127. Doll hats. Assorted sizes. Price per pair....$0.10

26128. Doll booties. Crocheted in wool. Price per pair.....$0.15

26129. Embroidered silk doll coat. Each.....$0.40

WILSON & SONS CATALOGUE No. 61

BABY DOLLS
ASSORTED SIZES

26130. Full-jointed dolls. Finest bisque head. Long baby dress. Price.....$0.85

26131. Superior quality dolls with bisque head, wool dress. Price.....$0.75

26132. Fine lace dress with silk bow. Price.....$0.50

26133. Large baby doll. Full bonnet with lace trim. Bisque head. Price.....$1.00

26134. Fine cloth body, simple bonnet. Price.....$0.70

PAPA DOLLS

26135. Dressed doll with bisque head and limbs. Finest checkered suit. Height: four inches. Price.....$1.25

26136. Same as above with top hat and overcoat. Price.....$2.00

MAMA DOLLS

26137. Finest muslin and lace dress. Bisque head with painted hair. Smooth finish. Bisque hands and legs. Price.....$1.50

26138. Other mama dolls with various styles in dresses and hair. Price.....$1.50 each

GIRL DOLLS

26139. Our most popular doll. Fine pink ribbon and painted yellow hair. Full lace sleeves and undertrimmings. Price.....$1.00

26140. Same as above, but with pink party outfit and yellow toy balloon. Price.....$1.25

BOY DOLLS

26141. Bisque head and limbs with fashionable sailor suit. Price.....$0.95

TINY BOOKS

26142. real bindings. Many titles. Set of ten. Price.....$0.75

We enclose 2 order blanks in each Catalogue sent you, and will furnish more on application, free. It is not absolutely necessary to have these blanks, but they are a great convenience and prevent many mistakes. If you do not happen to have any handy, try to conform to the sample heading here given, to prevent error: PLEASE SEND ORDER BLANK TO US AT ADDRESS FOUND ON REVERSE.

(kindly cut along the dotted line)

MESSRS. WILSON & SONS.
American distributors of British goods
Please send to
Name.....
Post Office.....
County.....
State.....

How to be shipped (See rules in Catalogue, Page 1).....
Enclosed please find $.....
The following items are selected from Catalogue No.....

No. of Article in Catalogue.	Quantity.	ARTICLES WANTED.	Sizes, Colors, etc.	Price.

Th

MEA

NEST

DO

L L

IN

THE

WO

RLD

Greatest!!!!!

THE ~~MEANEST~~ DOLL
IN THE WORLD

❧

By Ann M. Martin &
Laura Godwin

Pictures by
Brian Selznick

Hyperion Paperbacks for Children
New York

For Brian Selznick
—A.M.M. and L.G.

For Maureen Sullivan and Christine Kettner
—B.S.

Special thanks to Eileen Gilshian.
Special thanks to Robb Bennett, Ph.D.,
Seed Pest Management Officer, British Columbia Ministry of Forests,
for his help in unraveling the tangled world of spiders and their nests.

Text copyright © 2003 by Ann M. Martin and Laura Godwin
Illustrations copyright © 2003 by Brian Selznick

First Hyperion Paperback edition, 2005.
5 7 9 10 8 6

Printed in the United States of America

Library of Congress Cataloging-in-Publication Data on file.

ISBN 0-7868-5297-6 (pbk.)

Visit www.hyperionbooksforchildren.com

CONTENTS

I am Queen of all dolls!!!

CHAPTER ONE

Miami Beach-a-go-go

ANNABELLE DOLL sat in the soap dish high above the bathtub in the Palmers' house. Since Nora Palmer was just below her, taking a bath, Annabelle had to hold still, still, still. She could not be caught moving. But she was desperate to see the cause of all the splashing and shouting she heard.

"Shark! Shark attack!" cried Nora. "Look out, dollies. Get out of the way!"

There was a tremendous splash and the sound of sloshing as water hit the tile floor of the bathroom.

"Everyone out of the ocean!" commanded

Nora. "Come on, dollies. Come on back to the beach."

For a moment Annabelle heard nothing, even though she knew full well that the entire Funcraft family was in the tub. Like Annabelle, they could not laugh or talk or move about on their own. Not while Nora was in the room.

Annabelle thought longingly of the dollhouse, her nice quiet home. And of Kate Palmer, Nora's nine-year-old sister, the owner of the Doll family and their house. Kate never played wild noisy games with the Dolls. She merely posed them in the rooms of their ancient house, and occasionally talked to them or rearranged the furniture. But Nora, who was five, and the owner of the Funcrafts, invented games like Miami Beach-a-go-go and Rancher Family. She was only supposed to play those games with the Funcrafts, who were new and made of plastic. But often she crept into Kate's room and snatched up Annabelle and maybe one of the other Dolls— Mama or Papa or Nanny or Uncle Doll or Auntie Sarah or Bobby or Baby Betsy. And the next thing Annabelle knew, she was riding a hideous old plastic horse, or being driven into the bathroom in a Barbie car. Since the Dolls were over one hundred years old, made of china, and dressed in antique clothing trimmed with lace and ribbons, Nora's games could be dangerous.

However, Annabelle admitted, sometimes they looked exciting. And the Funcrafts certainly enjoyed them.

Annabelle decided she simply had to see what was going on in the water below her. Ever so slowly she pulled herself up straighter, then bent over a bit, just a teeny tiny bit, and slid her eyes downward.

Annabelle didn't know much about baths, but she was fairly certain that a person taking a bath was supposed to be naked, and Nora was not naked. She was wearing a flowered bathing suit, blue swimming goggles, and a pair of rubber flippers. Floating around her in the tub were part of her farm set (two cows, a chicken, and a sheep), six small boats, Tiffany Funcraft, who was Annabelle's best friend, and Tiffany's family—her brother Bailey, her mom, her dad, and Baby Britney. Nora had snapped off their plastic everyday clothes and

3

snapped on the contents of Funcraft Accessory Pack #214A. The dolls were now wearing bathing suits, caps, and sunglasses.

Annabelle couldn't be sure, but she thought the Funcrafts were smiling.

"Run for your lives, dollies!" said Nora suddenly, as she stood up in the tub. "It's a tidal wave."

Nora dropped into the water with an enormous splash, and the Funcrafts rode the crest of a wave from one end of the tub to another.

Annabelle felt foolish and unnecessary sitting high in the soap dish with no role in this game. True, Nora had stuck a paper cap and a little pair of sunglasses on her. But no part of Annabelle was plastic, and no part of

her belonged in water. If she were to fall into
the tub, her glue would unstick, her ribbons
would untie, and her clothing would probably
float away, maybe even go down the drain.

So Annabelle was relieved that Nora
knew enough to keep her dry. And she was
pleased at least to have been given the paper
cap and the glasses. But she didn't like

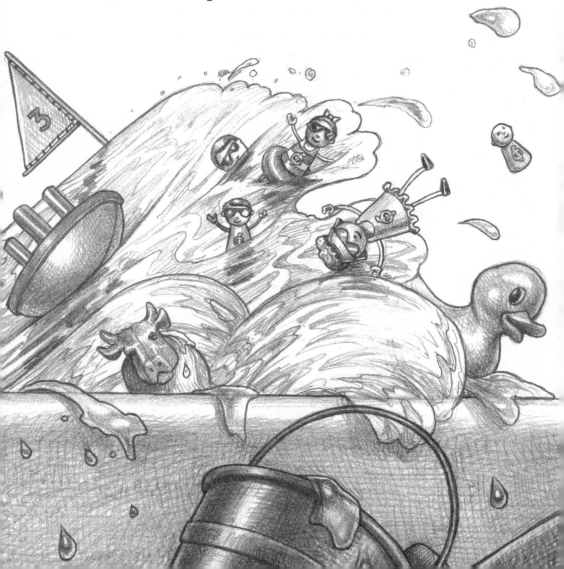

feeling silly and useless, watching from a distance while Tiffany floated and rode the waves. This was how it always was with Tiffany, though, thought Annabelle. It was one of the things that set her apart from her best friend.

Annabelle remembered the years and years and years when she had been the only living girl doll at 26 Wetherby Lane. Her family and their dollhouse had been shipped across the ocean from England to the United States in 1898 to be a present for a little girl named Gertrude, Kate's great-grandmother. Gertrude had grown up and had a daughter of her own—Kate's grandma Katherine, who lived with the Palmers—and then Katherine had had Annie, who was Kate's mother, and then Annie had had Kate and Nora. During all that time Annabelle had known no living dolls except the ones in her family.

"Why?" she used to ask her mother. "Why aren't there any other live dolls here?"

"Not all dolls take the oath," Mama would reply patiently. "The Doll Code of Honor is serious. A lot of responsibility comes with being a living doll. Many dolls choose to be regular everyday dolls."

"But not us," Annabelle had said.

"No, not us," Mama agreed.

Annabelle had lived in the humans' house for more than a hundred years before the Funcrafts arrived. She'd been glad she was a living doll, but sometimes she had felt lonely, especially after Auntie Sarah had disappeared. Annabelle loved her mother and her father. She loved her brother, Bobby, and their sister, Baby Betsy. (Baby Betsy was an enormous doll from a different doll set, but who cared?) She loved Nanny, who helped to take care of her and Bobby and Baby Betsy. And she loved Uncle Doll. But she had wished for another girl doll her own age, someone who could be her best friend. That was before she had met Tiffany.

This was what Annabelle was thinking when below her she heard a slap and a whoosh as Nora sat down hard in the tub, and suddenly she found herself eye to eye with Tiffany, who had been shot up in the air by the force of the water.

"Whoo-ee! Hi, Annabelle!" called Tiffany in a tiny doll voice that she knew Nora couldn't hear over the noise of her tidal waves. Then she dropped back into the tub.

Annabelle tried very hard not to laugh. What, she thought, would she do without Tiffany? The Funcrafts had lived at the Palmers' for less than a year, and already Annabelle couldn't think how she had managed to get along for an entire century without a best friend. True, for the first fifty-five years of that century Auntie Sarah had been around, and Annabelle's life had at least been interesting. Auntie Sarah liked to explore. She liked to leave the Dolls' house and investigate things in the larger world of the humans' house. She used to come back from her adventures

and tell Annabelle about history and current events and famous woman explorers and other things she had learned from listening to the radio or trying to get a peek at newspapers and magazines and library books.

But one day, almost forty-six years ago now, Auntie Sarah had left the dollhouse and hadn't returned. Annabelle's family had been too afraid to go searching for her.

"Doll State," Nanny would remind Annabelle.

Which always made Annabelle feel grumpy, probably because she had been in Doll State more often than any of the other Dolls. If a human saw a doll moving, or thought she saw one moving, then *poof!*—the doll was rendered motionless and lifeless, like an ordinary doll, for twenty-four hours. This meant that the Dolls felt free to move about only when they were absolutely *certain* they wouldn't be seen. It also meant that whenever Annabelle asked about going on a hunt for Auntie Sarah, the answer was no.

During the long lonely time when Auntie Sarah had been missing, Annabelle had sometimes wondered something horrible: she

had wondered if perhaps her aunt had been a little *too* careless and had landed not in Doll State, but in Permanent Doll State. Permanent Doll State, a phrase the grown-ups didn't even like to say very often, referred to the worst thing that could happen to a doll. Mama and Papa usually said "PDS" in a whisper and looked down at their shoes.

"There's no such thing," Bobby and Annabelle used to say bravely to one another. But they weren't sure. PDS, like Doll State, harkened back to the oath, the Doll Code of Honor, which was meant to protect and preserve the secret life of dolls.

"The code reminds us," Nanny would tell Annabelle and Bobby, "to be careful, and that there are consequences if we are not careful. We might be punished with Doll State. Or even," she would add, lowering her voice to a whisper, "PDS."

"Belly flop! Belly flop!" cried Nora from below, and Annabelle leaned over just far enough to see Nora stand up and drop Mom Funcraft down, down to the water, where she landed on her tummy with a small smack.

Annabelle settled back in the soap dish.

Her thoughts returned to the lonely years when Auntie Sarah was missing. Annabelle had been afraid she would never see her aunt again. She had even realized she could no longer remember her very well.

Then the Funcrafts had arrived and everything had changed.

The Funcrafts had been a birthday present for Nora when she turned five. Their big pink plastic house had been placed in Nora's bedroom, which was down the hall from Kate's. Before Annabelle knew it, she and Tiffany were sneaking back and forth between the two rooms whenever they felt it was safe to do so. It hadn't taken Annabelle long to tell her new friend about her missing aunt, and to show her Auntie Sarah's journal, which she

had recently discovered. If not for Tiffany and the journal, Annabelle now thought, Auntie Sarah might still be trapped in the attic.

Annabelle was about to recall that creepy night in the dim, musty attic, when suddenly the door to the bathroom flew open and banged against the wall. Kate stood in the entryway, hands on hips. She looked at the puddles of water, at Nora in her bathing suit and flippers and goggles, at the Funcrafts and the array of boats and animals in the tub. And then she caught sight of Annabelle in the soap dish, wearing the paper cap and the glasses.

"Nora!" exclaimed Kate. "What are you doing? It's almost your bedtime." Kate pulled the plug in the tub, and Annabelle heard the water begin to gurgle. "And what is Annabelle doing in here? She shouldn't be near the water. What if she fell in? She's not like your dollies, Nora."

No, thought Annabelle. I'm nothing like Tiffany.

Nora stood up in the tub, dripping water down onto the Funcrafts. "That's why she's sitting way up there," said Nora. "So she's out of the way. She's just watching."

Annabelle's porcelain face reddened. *Just watching.* Sometimes Annabelle felt that was the only thing she was any good at.

Kate leaned across the tub and gently reached for Annabelle. "Come on," she said. "It's your bedtime. I think I'm going to give you a quiet night tonight."

This meant, Annabelle knew, that after Kate had settled the Dolls in their beds she was going to close up the front of their house and lock the tiny heart-shaped padlock with its key. Kate didn't do this very often, and Annabelle was glad. While a night closed into their house gave the Dolls more freedom to move about and to talk, it also meant that Annabelle was locked in and Tiffany was locked out.

Annabelle sighed as she looked between Kate's fingers at the Funcrafts below. She saw that Tiffany had floated all the way to one end of the tub, and was smiling a teeny smile as she twirled around and around in the whirlpool over the drain. Tiffany probably didn't even realize that Annabelle was being taken away.

Annabelle sighed again, feeling very small and left out. But she made a decision. If she didn't like feeling left out, then she would do something about it. She just didn't know what that something would be.

CHAPTER TWO

A Mission

ANNABELLE WAS relieved when, the next morning, Kate remembered to open up the dollhouse before she left for school. Annabelle had enjoyed having a family sing-along the night before, and being able to chant "R-E-S-P-E-C-T!" a little more loudly than usual. But she had missed visiting with Tiffany.

Now, back on her bed where she had been placed by Kate after the soap-dish rescue, Annabelle lay quietly, listening to the morning sounds of the Palmers' house. She heard voices in the kitchen as Kate and Nora and

1 5

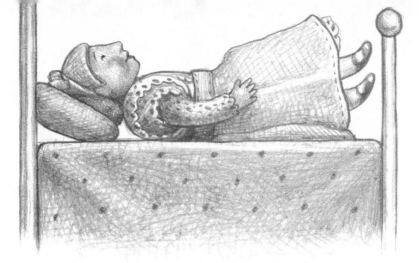

their parents and Grandma Katherine ate
breakfast. Then she heard doors open and
close as one by one the humans left the
house—Mr. and Mrs. Palmer went off to their
jobs, Kate left for fourth grade and Nora
for kindergarten, and finally Grandma
Katherine left to run errands.

"All clear?" Annabelle called a few
moments later.

"All clear," replied Papa Doll.

Annabelle leaped off of her bed and ran
down the stairs of the dollhouse to the first
floor. She sat at the edge of the parlor, her
legs dangling over the side. Far below her was
the floor of Kate's room.

"I wonder where Tiffany is," she said to
Auntie Sarah, who sat nearby, scribbling in
the pages of her journal. "She didn't try to
come over last night."

"Probably left behind in the bathtub," Auntie Sarah replied.

This was true. Poor Tiffany and her family, after enjoying games in the tub with Nora, were occasionally left there until the next time someone wanted to take a bath. And as fearless and talented as they were, they were not able to climb up the slippery sides of the tub to escape.

Annabelle was disappointed about Tiffany, but glad to have a moment with her aunt. She stood behind her and peered at the pages of the journal, the very same journal that Annabelle had found all those months ago, the clues in which had led her and Tiffany to the attic and the reunion with

Auntie Sarah. On its pages Auntie Sarah recorded her adventures and discoveries, most of which involved spiders—fascinating to Auntie Sarah and terrifying to Annabelle.

"What's that?" asked Annabelle, looking at her aunt's drawings of legs and eyes and abdomens. "*Amaurobius ferox?*" *Amaurobius ferox*, or the black lace weaver, was the spider for which Auntie Sarah had been searching when she had become trapped in the attic. Annabelle was pleased with herself for remembering its Latin name.

"No," replied Auntie Sarah, setting down the teeny fountain pen that had been added to the dollhouse in 1931. "This is a nursery web spider, *Dolomedes tenebrosus*. It's absolutely enormous. It's not seen very often, and it's partial to aquatic habitats, but it's native to eastern North America, and I'm determined to glimpse one with my own eyes someday. One never knows what one might find."

Annabelle shuddered. She didn't like pictures of spiders, let alone face-to-face meetings with live ones.

"I think I'll go on an Exploration to the

attic tonight, if that's possible," Auntie Sarah continued. "Would you and Tiffany like to come with me?"

An Exploration to look for an absolutely enormous, probably hairy spider? A Spider Hunt, really. Annabelle shuddered again. But she said bravely, "Sure."

If Auntie Sarah and Tiffany were going on a Spider Hunt, then Annabelle wanted to go with them.

The Dolls' house sat on a shelf in a corner of Kate's room. Below it was a small wooden stool, four steps high. When Kate was younger she had used the stool to reach the top floor of the house. She no longer needed it, but she left it there anyway, and Annabelle was glad. Without the stool, the Dolls would have been stranded in their home, high above the floor. With the stool, they could venture beyond Kate's room, which Annabelle and Auntie Sarah and Bobby did frequently. The other Dolls were content to stay put.

On the night after Miami Beach-a-go-go, Annabelle waited until she was sure the humans were in their beds and sound asleep.

Then she stood up from the uncomfortable position in which Kate had left her in the kitchen of the dollhouse and called to Auntie Sarah, who was lying on the dining room table.

"Can we go now?" she asked. She was determined to appear excited about the prospect of finding *Dolomedes tenebrosus*.

"I think so," replied Auntie Sarah. She slid stiffly off the table. "Let's go see if Tiffany is back in Nora's room."

Annabelle and her aunt called good-bye to the rest of the Dolls, made their way down the steps of the stool, and darted across the floor of Kate's darkened room. They were rounding the corner into the hallway when they heard a small shout. It was Tiffany.

"Hey!" she called. "Where are you going?"

"To the attic," replied Auntie Sarah. "On an Exploration. Can you join us?"

"Definitely." Tiffany took Annabelle's hand as they hurried along the hallway toward the attic door. "Nora didn't remember to take us out of the bathtub until tonight," she

said. "I love Miami Beach-a-go-go, but I don't know if it's worth getting stuck in the tub. What are we looking for in the attic?"

"*Dolomedes tenebrosus,*" Annabelle said proudly. "Right, Auntie Sarah?"

"That's right. *Dolomedes tenebrosus* is an especially large spider, Tiffany. It's mainly an outdoor spider, but does come inside occasionally. I think I might have seen one while I was stuck in the attic, but it's a little hard to tell. I was trapped there for such a long time. I never knew whether I was dreaming or . . ."

Auntie Sarah's voice trailed off, and Annabelle knew her aunt's mind had jumped to another topic. She said nothing, though, because they had reached the door to the attic, which was usually left ajar, and they needed to concentrate in order to pull it out far enough to slither through the opening. When they were on the other side of the door, they began the long climb up the stairs to the attic.

At the top, they lay together in a heap, panting. Each step was taller than the dolls, so the climb involved lots of pulling and pushing and puffing.

"All right," said Auntie Sarah after a few moments.

"All right," repeated Tiffany. "Now what does *Dola* . . . *Domi* . . . what does this spider look like?"

"It's enormous," said Annabelle.

"Yes, it's quite large. . . ." Auntie Sarah's voice trailed off again. "Girls, there's something else." She paused. "I've not mentioned this to anyone—"

"What? What is it?" cried Tiffany.

Annabelle, who had an idea that the something else concerned spiders, said nothing.

"Well, it's an idea I've been working on," said Auntie Sarah. "Come. Sit down with me."

Auntie Sarah led Annabelle and Tiffany through the dusty attic, which was lit only by a sliver of moonlight shining through the single small window on the far wall. They passed old cartons and discarded furniture and rolls of

2 2

carpet and finally stopped at a pile of rags. Auntie Sarah patted it. "Very comfy," she said.

The girls sat down, one on either side of Auntie Sarah.

Tiffany was wiggling with excitement. "What's your idea? What is it?"

"It is my dream," Auntie Sarah began slowly, "to start a spider farm."

"*What?*" cried Annabelle, leaping to her feet. She put a hand to her mouth.

"What do you want a spider farm for?" asked Tiffany reasonably.

"It has occurred to me," said Auntie Sarah, "that I could harvest the silk produced by spiders to make nearly invisible ropes and ladders and nets. Then even timid dolls like your parents, Annabelle, would feel more comfortable leaving the house. For instance, at times like last night when Kate locked us in we could still get outside. We could just lower a ladder—an almost invisible one—out a window, and climb down to the floor."

Annabelle stared at her aunt. She had to admit that this was a brilliant idea.

Auntie Sarah was just like all those famous women she was always telling Annabelle about—Madame Curie and Harriet Tubman and Amelia Earhart.

"Are you sure that would work?" asked Tiffany.

"Positive," replied Auntie Sarah. "Spider silk is extremely strong. A single strand of it can be stronger than a strand of steel. Plus, it's stretchier than nylon, so it would be good for nets."

"Wow," said Tiffany.

"Do you want *Dolomedes tenebrosus* for the farm?" asked Annabelle.

"No. I'm just curious about him. What I'd really like for the farm, at least in the beginning, is *Tegenaria domestica*. That's the most common house spider in America. He's a hard worker. Whenever his web is damaged, he immediately begins repairing it."

"Oh, so you could harvest lots and lots of the silk," said Annabelle.

"Exactly." Auntie Sarah smiled at her. "Later, once the farm has been established, I'll want to build up various herds, since different kinds of spiders produce different kinds of silk. But that's in the future. I plan to start small and grow. Also, I want to study spiders up close to find out how they're able to crawl straight up doors and walls, and how they dangle from high places. Just think—if dolls could do that! Imagine the benefit to dollkind."

"If there were doll history books," said Annabelle, "you'd be in the chapter about amazing women. Maybe you'd have a chapter all to yourself." Annabelle felt suddenly braver. After all, she was the niece of her very brave aunt.

"Let's get started!" exclaimed Tiffany, standing up. "So, are we going to look for that huge spider, or are we going to do something about the farm?"

"Both," replied Auntie Sarah. "What I'd like to do tonight is keep a log of all the spiders we see. I want to get an idea of how many kinds are up here, for one thing. If we do spot *Dolomedes tenebrosus*, well, that would be a cause for celebration. So let's start looking. Call me even if you see a spiderweb. I can tell by the web what kind of spider made it."

Tiffany and Annabelle and her aunt split

up and started searching the dark corners and hidey-holes of the attic. Every few moments someone would call out, "Here's a web!" or "What kind of spider is this?" or "I see something over there." And Auntie Sarah would investigate and make notes in her journal.

Much later, Annabelle was noticing that the light in the attic was growing stronger, when two things happened at once.

Tiffany said, "Gosh, I think it's getting late. We'd better start back downstairs."

And Auntie Sarah said, "Oh, my heavens. I do believe that's the web of *Dolomedes tenebrosus.*"

"Where?" cried Annabelle. "There?"

"Yes," said Auntie Sarah, sounding greatly excited.

And Annabelle, determined to show Tiffany and her aunt that she wasn't afraid of enormous spiders, ran across the attic floor, stumbled on a scrap of carpet, and fell headlong into the web. "Uh-oh," she said as she sat up. She began to pull at the sticky wisps of silk that covered her face and hair and clothing.

The web was ruined.

"Oh. Oh, I'm sorry, Auntie Sarah."

Auntie Sarah pressed her hands together and said briskly, "It's all right, Annabelle. What's done is done."

Annabelle got to her feet. Tiffany and Auntie Sarah were staring at her. They stood just inches away, but for a moment Annabelle felt as if she were high in the soap dish again, set apart from the others who were playing below.

CHAPTER THREE

A Close Call

EVEN THOUGH GOING down the stairs was easier than going up, the dolls had to take their time. The attic stairs were not carpeted, so Annabelle and Tiffany and Auntie Sarah moved quietly and cautiously. Every time Annabelle looked at the floor below, she couldn't help but worry what would happen if she were to slip and fall the rest of the way down. She didn't mention this, though, as brave Auntie Sarah and Tiffany scrambled ahead of her.

When they reached the bottom, Annabelle peered around the door. "It must be later than we think," she whispered. "There's a lot of light in the hallway."

"Hmm. By my calculations it couldn't be later than five o'clock," said Auntie Sarah.

"Five o'clock!" exclaimed Annabelle. "We were supposed to be home by four. Mama and Papa—"

Tiffany gave Annabelle a little push into the hall. "Well, let's not waste time talking about it," she said. "Hurry up. Run!"

Annabelle and Tiffany ran into the hallway ahead of Auntie Sarah. They had just passed Nora's room when Annabelle screeched to a halt and let out a small shriek.

"What's wrong?" asked Tiffany.

"I heard something!"

And at that moment, Annabelle, staring ahead of her, saw a pair of bare feet step from Kate's room into the hall. She almost shrieked again, but Tiffany clapped a hand over her mouth. Annabelle looked wildly around. Auntie Sarah had ducked back behind the attic door. Annabelle could see her shoes beneath it. The door to Kate's room was a few feet ahead. On the floor

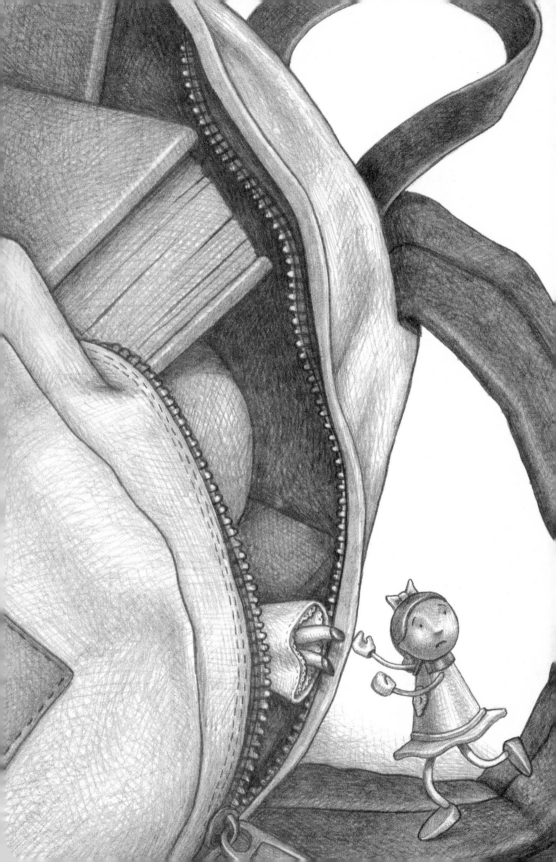

outside of it, just inches from the dolls, was Kate's backpack.

"Quick!" said Tiffany in a loud whisper. "The attic!"

"No, she'll see us!" Annabelle saw Tiffany's eyes jump hopefully to Nora's doorway. "We can't go there either," said Annabelle. She was feeling panicky. The bare feet were moving sleepily along the hallway, closer and closer. In a flash Annabelle grabbed Tiffany by the wrist and yanked her toward the backpack. "In here," she said.

Annabelle dove headfirst into the largest compartment of the backpack with Tiffany just behind her. She tried not to squeal as she sat on something sharp, then felt Tiffany land on her head. The girls huddled together, breathing heavily and listening to the sounds from the hallway. They heard Kate's footsteps pad into the bathroom. Then the bathroom door was closed gently.

"Safe!" exclaimed Tiffany softly. "That was a close call. Good thinking, Annabelle."

"Thank you. I hope Auntie Sarah saw us hide in here," Annabelle whispered. She frowned. "How on earth could she have made such a mistake? If Kate is already up it must be much later than five."

"Well, we can't worry about that now," replied Tiffany. "We have to figure out what to do. Do you think we have time to get out of here?"

Annabelle didn't have a chance to answer. The girls heard the bathroom door open again. "Okay, as soon as Kate goes back to her room," Tiffany said quickly, "we'll climb out and run into Nora's room. She's probably still asleep. You can hide with my family, and we'll just have to hope Kate won't notice you're missing from—"

"Shh," hissed Annabelle suddenly. "Shh, SHH!"

Tiffany stopped talking as a hand appeared above the backpack and with a loud *Z-I-I-I-P*, closed it up, leaving Annabelle and Tiffany in darkness. Annabelle grabbed for Tiffany's hand and held it tightly. Then the backpack was swooped into the air and Annabelle felt Kate wrap her arms around it. She and Tiffany bumped up and down as Kate carried the backpack . . . where?

"Where are we going?" whispered Tiffany.

"Shh," was all Annabelle would reply.

A few seconds later the backpack was dropped to the floor. Annabelle crashed against Tiffany, but remained silent. The girls listened hard. They heard Kate's radio playing. They heard drawers opening and closing, and small thumps and clatters as Kate got ready for school. And all the while Annabelle hoped that the following things would happen: that Kate would partially open the backpack, and that she would then forget what she was doing, abandon it, and go downstairs for breakfast, at which point Annabelle and Tiffany would crawl out and go to their homes. They would have to admit to their parents what had happened, of course, but since Annabelle held Auntie Sarah responsible, she wasn't too worried about this.

However, none of those things happened. Kate left the backpack closed, and presently she slung it up again and carried it downstairs. With a small thump she deposited it on the floor. In the kitchen? In the hallway?

Kitchen, Annabelle decided as she heard clinkings and clankings and smelled toast and eggs. Annabelle wanted desperately to talk to Tiffany, but she knew better. It was a miracle that she and Tiffany weren't already in Doll State.

The clinkings and clankings grew louder, and Annabelle heard voices. Soon the entire Palmer family had gathered for breakfast. Just when the noise in the kitchen became so loud that Annabelle wanted to put her hands over her ears, she felt Tiffany nudge her. Annabelle

nudged
her back.
"Annabelle,"
Tiffany whispered
urgently.

"SHH!"

"Oh, they can't
hear us. Not with all
that racket. . . .
Annabelle?"

"What?"

"I'm sitting in gum."

"Gum? Are you sure?"

"Yes! I'm stuck in it. I can't
move."

Annabelle got to her feet carefully
and held out her hand to Tiffany. "Here.
Let me pull you up."

Tiffany took Annabelle's hand.
Annabelle pulled. And pulled. And pulled.
"I . . . can't . . . pull . . . any . . ." she said,
puffing, and at that moment, Tiffany suddenly flew toward her. The girls fell against
the edge of a book.

They hugged each other nervously, but all
they heard was the sound of chairs being

pushed back and voices calling good-bye as Kate's mother and father left for their jobs. And then . . . "Nora, hurry up!" called Kate as once again the backpack was lifted into the air.

Annabelle heard Grandma Katherine say, "Here, Kate. Let me help you with that," and she and Tiffany were jostled about as Kate struggled to put her arms through the straps of the backpack.

"Oh, there you are," said Kate a moment later. "Come on, Nora, let's go."

"Good-bye, girls," said Grandma Katherine. "See you later."

"Bye!" Kate and Nora called back.

A door closed, and Annabelle Doll was Outdoors.

She couldn't help whispering to Tiffany. "We're outdoors. *Outdoors.* I've never, ever been outdoors. I mean, not since our packing carton was delivered to Gertrude, and that was over a hundred years ago."

Tiffany gripped Annabelle's hand even harder. "I think we're going to *school*," she said.

Bump, bump, bump. Kate Palmer ran. She skipped. She plopped down on the sidewalk and retied her sneaker. She played a game of hopscotch with Nora when they found a hopscotch court chalked onto the sidewalk near school. Every time Kate moved, Annabelle and Tiffany were bounced or jostled or thrown from side to side. It was a horribly uncomfortable ride, and yet . . . Annabelle had to admit that it was an exciting adventure.

"Nora," said Kate suddenly, "I want to save my hopscotch rock. Can you put it in my backpack for me?"

"Sure," replied Nora, and the backpack was unzipped and a small rock was tossed inside. It tumbled through the heap of books and papers and settled in Tiffany's lap.

"Thanks," said Kate.

Nora didn't bother to zip the backpack closed, and a small amount of sunlight filtered down to Annabelle. She looked around. She was sitting on the edge of a paperback book. *"Mary Poppins,"* she whispered as she read the writing on the spine. Next to her was a pencil covered with tooth marks, the eraser chewed off. On the other side of the pencil was Tiffany. Her legs were tucked under a piece of paper, the rock resting in her lap.

"Help get this off me," Tiffany hissed. "It weighs a ton."

As Annabelle huffed and pushed, Kate let out a yell. "Harmoni! Ayanna! Hi!" And then, "Hi, Rachel!"

Kate stood still for a moment. "All right, Nora. There's Martha. You walk with her to your classroom. Grandma Katherine will pick you up when kindergarten's over, okay?"

"Okay. Bye, Kate."

Annabelle heard Nora's footsteps running off. And then she heard so many voices all at once that she couldn't even tell who was talking:

"Kate, look what Harmoni got yesterday."

"I didn't finish our reading homework. Did you, Rachel?"

"The science fair is coming up."

"Oh, no, there's Francine. Don't let her see us!"

With this, the backpack lurched as Kate broke into a run. For a few minutes all Annabelle heard was heavy panting and the sound of running feet. Presently the light in the backpack grew dimmer and the noises changed from outdoor sounds to a roar of loud voices. Annabelle smelled new smells, smells she couldn't quite identify. She looked up and saw a beige ceiling lurch by, dotted with dim lights.

"Tiffany," she dared to whisper. "I think we're in Kate's school."

"Who's Francine?" asked Tiffany.

"That girl Kate's always talking about.

The
one—"
The backpack
suddenly tipped from
side to side, then was
dropped to the ground.
Annabelle looked up just in
time to see Kate's hand reaching
down. It nearly closed around
Tiffany, who leaped aside and
squeezed herself into a far
corner of the backpack. The
hand grabbed up the hopscotch
rock, then withdrew, then reached in
again and pulled out a notebook. And then
the backpack was hoisted high in the air where
it came to rest on something hard.

"Look, Ayanna," said Kate. "I found this
rock . . ."

Kate's voice trailed off as a bell rang loudly. The roar of voices grew dimmer until finally Annabelle heard . . . nothing.

"What happened? Where is everybody?" asked Tiffany.

"In their classrooms," replied Annabelle importantly. For years she had heard tales about school—first from Gertrude, then from Katherine, then from Annie, and now from Kate.

Tiffany knew very little about school. "Where are we?" she asked.

"Maybe over Kate's coat hook?"

Annabelle and Tiffany waited. When they had heard nothing for several minutes, Tiffany dared to paw through the things in the backpack and peer through the opening in the zipper.

"What do you see?" asked Annabelle.

"A long, long, long room. The hallway, I guess. It's lined with coats hanging on hooks. And there are these shelves above the hooks and I can see lunches and backpacks and sneakers and things on them. And on the floor under the coat hooks are more back-packs and sneakers."

"Are there any people in the hall?"

"Nope."

"Where are we?" asked Annabelle.

"On one of the shelves."

"Oh." Annabelle got to her feet and stood next to Tiffany, peeking through the opening. "Just think," she said. "We can spend all day watching from here and no one will see us. When we get home we'll be able to tell everyone what school is like."

"We could tell them even more if we could visit the classrooms."

"Oh, well," said Annabelle.

"We ought to have enough time," murmured Tiffany, looking down.

"For what?"

"An Exploration in school."

"Oh, Tiffany, we can't!"

"Why not? We have all day. I don't want to be stuck here for hours and hours. We can sneak out and look around, then get in Kate's back-pack again before school's over."

"But, Tiffany, look how high up we are. How are we going to get down to the floor?"

"Oh, I'm sure there's a way," Tiffany replied, sticking her head through the opening. "Now you see? This is exactly what your aunt's spider farm would be good for. We need one of those ladders she was talking about."

"Oh, well," said Annabelle again.

"But we don't have one, so we'll just have to figure something else out. Come on, Annabelle."

Annabelle climbed out of the backpack after Tiffany and sat on the edge of the shelf.

"Okay," said Tiffany. "We'll slide down the straps of the backpack to Kate's coat, and then crawl down the coat until we can drop to the floor."

Annabelle said nothing.

"Come on, we have to go. When are we ever going to be in school again?

This is a once-in-a-lifetime opportunity. You're not going to let it go by, are you?"

And Annabelle, picturing herself sitting alone in the soap dish, said, "No. I'm not. Okay. Let's go."

CHAPTER FOUR

The Dolls at School

AS ANNABELLE sat on the edge of
the shelf and looked down to the floor, she
decided that possibly this was the most afraid
she had ever been. She was more afraid than
when The Captain, the Palmers' cat, had
snatched Papa Doll and run away with him.
(After that, The Captain had been banished
to the first floor of the house.) She was more
afraid than when she and Tiffany,
during their hunt for Papa, had decided to
search The Captain's bed. And she was more
afraid than when, decades ago, Grandma
Katherine, six years old, had painted

Annabelle's hair green. Annabelle's hair was still green, which Annabelle didn't mind. But she had been terribly concerned that green hair might be a cause for Doll State. (Apparently it wasn't, but one never knew.)

"Come on, Annabelle," said Tiffany. She had already slid halfway down one of the straps of the backpack, and now her dangling feet hovered just an inch above Kate's coat. "Let me help you."

"No, no," said Annabelle quickly. "I can do it myself."

And she did. Annabelle didn't give herself time to think about what she was doing. She didn't look down, either. She fixed her eyes on the school ceiling, gripped the strap, and, hand over hand, worked her way to the end.

"You did it!" cried Tiffany. "Now let go. You'll land on the coat."

Annabelle squeezed her eyes shut and let go. She felt the collar of Kate's coat beneath her feet.

"Good," said Tiffany. "Now we just crawl down the coat. Here, you can grab on to the buttons." In no time Annabelle and Tiffany

had reached the bottom of Kate's coat.
They were still almost a foot above the
floor. "Ready? Drop," said Tiffany, and
she dropped, landing with a little thump.

"I can't drop!" exclaimed
Annabelle, finally looking down.
"I'll break when I land. Remember what happened when
we were rescuing Papa and he
had to jump to the floor? He
broke his leg. Plus, how are we
going to get back up later? Did
you think of that?" When
Annabelle was scared, she felt
cranky.

Tiffany glanced around. She
spied a scarf lying on the floor nearby.
"Okay, land on this." She dragged the
scarf under Annabelle and heaped it
into a little mountain. "We can use it
again later to climb up to Kate's
coat."

"If it's still here," Annabelle
muttered. But she dropped and
landed safely, then slithered to the
floor.

49

Tiffany looked at her hopefully.

"Okay, this is really great," admitted Annabelle. She looked all the way up the hall in one direction, and all the way down it in the other. "School, Tiffany. Can you believe it?"

Tiffany grinned. "What should we do first?"

"Let's find Kate's classroom," said Annabelle. "Maybe we can hide somewhere and watch Kate and her friends, see what they do all day in school."

"Yeah, maybe we'll even learn something. Nanny would approve of that."

"There are so many doors, though," said Annabelle. "One after another. They must be doors to classrooms, but how do we know which class is Kate's?"

Tiffany thought for a moment. "We don't," she said. "But we'll follow SELMP rules."

SELMP. Annabelle hadn't thought about SELMP in several months. She and Tiffany had formed SELMP, the Society for Exploration and the Location of Missing Persons, shortly before Papa had disappeared in the jaws of The Captain. Through SELMP, they had found Papa. And then they had found Auntie Sarah in the attic where she had been trapped for so long. But after that, Annabelle and Tiffany hadn't had much use for SELMP.

"Perfect!" cried Annabelle. If ever a proper Exploration were needed, now was it.

"We'll investigate each classroom as we come to it," said Tiffany. "If we see Kate inside, we'll look for a hiding place. If we don't see her, we'll move on to the next room."

"And while we're in the hallway, we should stay close to the walls. There are plenty of boots and things to hide behind if somebody comes by."

"Okay," said Tiffany.

The nearest door was just a few feet away from where Annabelle and Tiffany had landed. They crept by shoes and boots and book bags and backpacks. When they reached the door, they peered around the corner.

"Wow—" Annabelle started to say, but Tiffany poked her, and held her finger to her lips.

Through the years, as Annabelle had listened to bedtime stories read to Kate and Annie and Katherine and Gertrude, she had heard lots of descriptions of class- rooms. She expected to see a wooden desk for the teacher at the front of the room, a blackboard behind it, and twenty or thirty student desks arranged in neat rows. What she saw in this room was a teacher's desk, just as she had imagined, but the board behind it was green, and the desks for the students were grouped together in fours and fives to make tables. And all around the room were so many other things that Annabelle gasped as she tried to take them all in—draw- ings and posters and charts and maps on the walls, an aquarium full of fish, a cage labeled ETHEL with a guinea pig inside, a cage labeled ECHO with a parakeet inside, a shelf of books, three bean-bag chairs, displays and art projects and a xylophone and plants in pots and board games and a jar full of pennies.

Annabelle looked for so long at the things in the room that she almost forgot to look for Kate, and she jumped a little when Tiffany pulled her back into the hallway and said, "I didn't see her."

"Um, I didn't either," said Annabelle guiltily. Then she added, "School looks like fun."

Tiffany nodded. "I feel sorry for Ethel, though. I wonder how she lost her tail. I've never seen a kitten without a tail."

"Ethel is a *guinea pig*, Tiffany."

"That's a pig?"

"Well, not a pig like on a farm. A guinea pig— Never mind. I'll explain later. Come on."

Annabelle and Tiffany scurried down the hall to the next door and peeked inside. This classroom looked very much like the last one, but the students in it were older. Kate was not among them, though.

"Okay. Next room," said Tiffany.

The girls ran ahead, but came to a stop when the hall suddenly widened. They saw a tall window on one side, a closed door on the other, and a large plaque on the wall that read

FRIENDSHIP,
RESPECT, TRUST,
RESPONSIBILITY,
KINDNESS —
WE ARE PROUD
OF OUR SCHOOL

"What is this place?" asked Tiffany.

"I think it's a lobby," replied Annabelle.

"There's nowhere to hide here."

"But there are classrooms ahead. I can hear voices."

"What should we do?"

Annabelle felt brave. "Run for it!" she cried.

The girls plunged through the lobby, relieved that the walls of coat hooks and shelves continued on the other side. They passed an open door with the words LOST AND FOUND printed on it.

"Remember when Kate lost her sneakers and then she found them in the Lost and Found?" asked Annabelle. "I guess this is where they were." Annabelle eyed the enormous wire bin that was brimming over with hats and jackets and shoes and books and toys. "I don't know how anybody would find anything in there, though."

"It helps to be taller," said Tiffany.

No one was in the hall, so the girls continued running until they came to a classroom door. They had barely peeked inside when Annabelle gasped, grasped Tiffany, and pulled her behind a pair of boots.

"What?" exclaimed Tiffany.

"Nora! Didn't you see her? She was playing right near the door. This must be one of the kindergarten rooms. We don't want Nora to see us at school. I think we should go back through the lobby to the other part of the school. That's where the older kids are."

"Okay, but let's check the room across the hall before we go back. Just to make sure."

"All right."

Annabelle and Tiffany were peeping into the other classroom when Annabelle heard voices and footsteps in the hall. She looked over her shoulder. Two grown-up humans were just inches away. And this time there were no convenient boots nearby. In a panic, Annabelle pushed Tiffany inside the classroom, and the girls scurried into the bottom shelf of a bookcase. A moment later four feet stepped into the room.

"Wow, I never heard them coming," whispered Tiffany.

"Me neither. We have to be much more careful." Annabelle peered around the classroom. "I'm pretty sure this is another kindergarten," she said.

The kids in this room looked about Nora's age. And there were no desks except for the teacher's. Instead, at one end of the room were two long tables lined with small chairs. From other smaller tables scattered about the room hung signs that said OUR BEAN PLANTS, HOW MANY IS 100?, BUILD YOUR OWN CITY, COOKING TIME, and MEET OUR GOLD-FISH. In one corner of the room was a mountain of blocks. And not far from Annabelle and Tiffany were a wooden stove, a wooden sink, a box of dressing-up clothes, a dollhouse, and quite a few dolls, large and small.

"Tiffany," whispered Annabelle, "you don't suppose those dolls are—"

"Alive?" Tiffany whispered back. "Oh, I hope not."

Most of the dolls were not properly dressed. One had been shoved headfirst into the sink. And a girl and a boy were playing with two others in a way that looked to Annabelle to be quite uncivilized.

"How are we going to get out of here?" Annabelle asked. She turned her attention back to the adult feet nearby.

"As soon as the grown-ups leave, we'll leave too," said Tiffany.

"Okay." Annabelle crept between two books and settled in to watch the feet. She was about to tell Tiffany to hide with her when she heard a shout.

"Hey! Hey!" cried a girl. "Look, Henry! I see a new doll!"

In a flash, a hand had reached for the shelf and whisked Tiffany into the air. Annabelle slid farther back between the books. She didn't let Tiffany out of her sight, though.

"Jenna, can I play with it?" asked Henry.

It, thought Annabelle.

"No, I saw it. I want to play with it first. Then you can have a turn."

As Annabelle watched, Jenna carried Tiffany to a small rocking chair and plopped down in it. She reached for a baby bonnet. And then, as Jenna untied the ribbons of the bonnet, Annabelle saw Tiffany pinch Jenna's arm.

Annabelle's eyes widened as Jenna dropped Tiffany and stared at her. But then she shouted, "Henry!"

Annabelle sighed and looked at the clock on the wall. Nine-thirty. Doll State lasts twenty-four hours. Tiffany was going to be stuck here in

Doll State until nine-thirty the next morning. Should Annabelle stay with her? Should
she try to go home by herself?

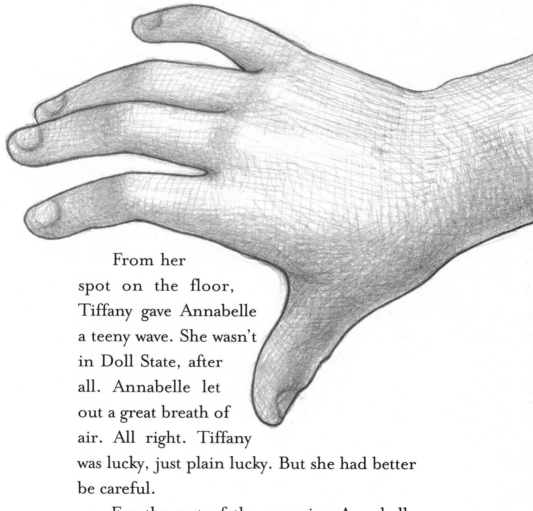

From her
spot on the floor,
Tiffany gave Annabelle
a teeny wave. She wasn't
in Doll State, after
all. Annabelle let
out a great breath of
air. All right. Tiffany
was lucky, just plain lucky. But she had better
be careful.

For the rest of the morning Annabelle
watched as Henry pushed Tiffany across the
floor in a plastic school bus, as two girls put

Tiffany to bed in the dollhouse, as a boy tucked Tiffany in his pocket and read a book to her, and finally as a girl with lots and lots of braids in her hair grabbed 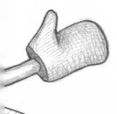 Tiffany and exclaimed, "My dolly!" All the while Annabelle tried to think of something to do.

At 11:20 a bell rang, and moments later the children in the room were lining up at the door.

"Good-bye," said the teacher. "Remember that tomorrow is Show and Share day." Annabelle had stood up and moved to the front of the shelf again. She peered from between the books. And she saw that the girl with the braids still clutched Tiffany in her hand.

"Good-bye, Mrs. Eckardt," said the girl.

"Good-bye," replied Mrs. Eckardt. And then she spied Tiffany. "Sophie, you know that the toys have to stay in our classroom.

Please leave the doll here. You can play with her tomorrow."

Annabelle watched as Sophie ran to the dollhouse and tossed Tiffany inside, then joined the end of the line of kids and marched into the hallway. A minute later the classroom was empty except for Mrs. Eckardt. Tiffany, lying on her back in the dollhouse, looked miles away from Annabelle.

Mrs. Eckardt sat at her desk and wrote in a notebook. Annabelle wished she would leave the classroom, but she did not. And after a few more minutes another bell rang, and soon the room was full of the afternoon kindergartners. For the next several hours Annabelle stayed in her hiding place and kept her eye on Tiffany. The after-noon kindergartners found her almost immediately, and played with her as the morning kindergartners had. When the last bell of the day rang, at 2:40, the children left the room and Mrs. Eckardt left with them.

Annabelle waited until the room had been quiet for five full minutes. Then she approached Tiffany, who was sitting on a blanket on the floor by the dollhouse.

For a moment the girls stared at one another. Finally Annabelle said, "School's over. Kate has gone home by now."

"I know," replied Tiffany.

Annabelle wanted to cry.

CHAPTER FIVE

Ms. Feldman Rules!

THE NIGHT THAT Annabelle and Tiffany spent in Kate's school was like no other Annabelle could remember. At first, Annabelle could do nothing but worry. She worried that Kate would notice she was missing. She worried that Nora would notice Tiffany was missing. She worried about what the humans would think, and whether the rest of their families could go into Doll State because of what the girls had done. And of course she worried about the Dolls and the Funcrafts, certain they would be terrified, although, as Tiffany pointed out, Auntie

Sarah must have seen the girls disappear into the backpack. She would be able to figure out where they were.

Eventually, Annabelle managed to stop worrying. Once she and Tiffany were certain the building was empty, Tiffany drove them through the hallways in a wooden dump truck they borrowed from Mrs. Eckardt's room. They investigated the cafeteria, the gym, the nurse's office, and Principal Hale's office. They read some books in the library. They looked at each other through a magnifying glass in Room 201. They shouted and sang as loudly as they pleased.

At last, though, they decided to locate Kate's room. They wanted to be able to watch Kate arrive the next morning. When they finally came across a classroom with a display of family photos on the bulletin board, and saw a picture of Kate and Nora and their parents and Grandma Katherine, they knew they were in the right place. They looked around until they found a cardboard carton. It was labeled MISC., it had no lid, and it was full of dusty papers and rubber bands and pencils and boxes of chalk. Best of all, several small holes had been poked in the sides, perfect for seeing without being seen. The girls didn't know what MISC. meant, but decided it probably wasn't important. So they crawled into the carton and settled down for the night.

In the morning they watched as the darkness in the room lightened to gray, and then as sunshine crept in. Pretty soon, thought Annabelle, Kate will be here. Annabelle knew she would feel better just seeing Kate.

The clock on the wall said 8:00 exactly when Annabelle heard footsteps in the hall. She nudged Tiffany. A moment later a tall woman carrying a Thermos and two heavy tote bags walked into the room and set her things down on the teacher's desk.

"That must be Ms. Feldman," Annabelle whispered to Tiffany. She looked at Ms.

Feldman with interest. Kate claimed to love her fourth-grade teacher. Annabelle had heard Kate tell Grandma Katherine that Ms. Feldman was nice and fair and not mean and always listened and didn't have a teacher's pet. And also that she thought up fun projects for Kate and her classmates.

The dolls watched as Ms. Feldman poured herself a cup of coffee from the Thermos, then worked at her desk. After a while she stood up, and wrote a list of words on the green chalkboard behind her. She found a book and marked a place in it. She fed a hamster playing in a cage near her desk. She had pulled a sheaf of papers out of a folder and was starting to read them when Annabelle heard noisy voices in the hallway. Ms. Feldman glanced up.

"Hi, Ms. Feldman!" called two boys as they ran into the classroom.

"Good morning, James. Good morning, Ben. Are you ready to start our new project today?"

"Yes," replied James, "and I know who I'm going to interview. My great-aunt Bess. She used to play *baseball*."

Three more children entered the room then. Annabelle looked eagerly for Kate. She squirmed and wiggled.

"What are you doing?" whispered Tiffany. "Hold still."

"I'm just trying to see. Where's Kate?"

"She'll be here."

Annabelle watched as three more boys and four girls entered the room. No Kate.

"Where is she?" asked Annabelle.

And suddenly there was Kate. She skipped into the room with two other girls.

"Good morning, Kate. Good morning, Harmoni. Good morning, Ayanna," said Ms. Feldman.

"Harmoni and Ayanna! Those girls are Harmoni and Ayanna!" exclaimed Annabelle.

"Annabelle," Tiffany hissed. "You really, really have to be quiet. Someone's going to hear us. You don't want to go into Doll State today, do you? If that happened, we'd be stuck here for three more days, because today is Friday, and you wouldn't come around until tomorrow, which would be Saturday, and—"

"Okay, okay," said Annabelle. But she

didn't feel grumpy. Only excited about finally seeing Kate. And seeing her outside the house on Wetherby Lane. This was such a wonderful opportunity that Annabelle even forgot about her family, who, she was certain, must be very, very worried back home in the dollhouse.

Through the hole in the box, Annabelle saw Kate sit at her desk, and put some papers and books inside it. Then she pulled something out of her pocket, leaned over, and tapped Harmoni, who was sitting at the next desk.

"Cool!" said Harmoni.

"Oh, cool," said Ayanna, as she joined them.

"Oh, cool," said a singsong voice from behind them.

Kate, Harmoni, and Ayanna turned around sharply, and Kate stuck her hand back in her pocket.

"Go away, Francine," said Ayanna.

Annabelle nudged Tiffany, who nodded. Here was awful Francine. She didn't look awful, though, Annabelle thought. Just like any other kid in the room.

"Nice socks," Francine said to Kate.

"Where did they come from? The baby department?"

"No!" exclaimed Kate. "They—"

"Francine, could I see you at my desk for a minute?" asked Ms. Feldman.

Francine made a face at Kate, then approached the teacher's desk. "Yes, Ms. Feldman?" she said sweetly.

Ms. Feldman looked gravely at Francine. "I am thinking of something that is in the lobby of our school," she said. "Something on the wall. Do you know what that is?"

Francine screwed up her face. For a moment, Annabelle thought she might give Ms. Feldman a smart answer, like "paint." But finally she said, "Our pride sign."

"That's right. Tell me what's on our pride sign, please."

Francine let out a great sigh. " 'Friendship, respect, trust, responsibility, kindness,' " she recited.

"Yes. And when I hear you speaking to your classmates the way you spoke to Kate just now, I think you have forgotten about the sign. And about our class friendship rules. How do you think Kate feels when you talk to her like that? Did she look happy?"

"No," replied Francine. Ms. Feldman didn't say anything, so finally Francine added, "She looked like her feelings were hurt."

"And hurting someone's feelings on purpose is not allowed in this room. Please remember that, Francine."

"Okay."

Annabelle watched, fascinated. No wonder Kate sometimes said, "Ms. Feldman rules!"

Tiffany was also watching, of course, and now she turned to Annabelle in the box,

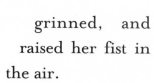

grinned, and
raised her fist in
the air.

Ms. Feldman
called Kate to her desk
too, then. "Kate," she said,
"Francine has something to say
to you."

"I'm sorry, Kate," said Francine.

Annabelle thought Francine sounded
like Talkin' Tammy, a doll Nora used to
own. (She had not been a living doll, thank
goodness.) When Nora pulled a string in
the back of Talkin' Tammy's neck, the doll
said "I'm hungry" or "Nighty-night" or "Bye-
bye" or "I love you"—all in the same flat, dull
voice.

"Francine doesn't mean it," Annabelle
whispered to Tiffany. "I wonder why she's so
nasty."

"She's a bully," Tiffany replied.

A bell rang then, causing Annabelle to
jump slightly. Ms. Feldman called the class to
order, and Annabelle and Tiffany spent the
next few hours watching Kate and learning
about nouns and the Thirteen Colonies and

tall tales and multiplication. Annabelle was wriggling with excitement again. She wished she could somehow attend a school for dolls. She knew that if she could go to school she would never be bored again. She wished too that Auntie Sarah were with her. Auntie Sarah would love fourth grade.

All the same, when another bell rang later in the morning and Kate's class left their room for lunch and recess, Annabelle and Tiffany lost no time scrambling out of the carton. Watching Kate in school was great, but Annabelle was desperate to see her family again.

Kate's room was now empty and silent. Ms. Feldman had even turned out the lights as she followed her class into the hall.

"The coast is clear," whispered Tiffany.

"Okay. But stick to the walls in case we have to hide suddenly," said Annabelle.

As quickly as they could, Annabelle and Tiffany made their way to the door of the room. They peeked into the hallway. Quiet. So once again, they snuck through the little tunnel between the wall and the shoes and book bags and backpacks on the floor.

"All right," said Tiffany. "Now comes the hard part. We have to cross the hallway. Kate's things are over there."

Annabelle looked up and down the hall. "Okay, go!" she cried.

The dolls dashed across the open space to the other side of the hall.

"Look!" said Tiffany, when they had safely reached the opposite wall. "The scarf is still there."

"Perfect," replied Annabelle.

She and Tiffany stood on top of the scarf. Above them was a coat, and above that, the dangling straps of a backpack.

"Okay, up we go," said Tiffany.

The dolls reached up and grabbed the bottom of the coat more easily than Annabelle had thought would be possible.

Kate must have worn a different coat today, Annabelle decided. This one didn't have as many buttons. But it had enough, just enough to allow Annabelle and Tiffany to scramble upward. When the dolls reached the collar of the coat they grabbed the straps of the backpack and began to climb them. They had almost reached the tops of the straps when a bell rang and suddenly the hallway was flooded with children and teachers.

"Quick!" cried Annabelle, alarmed. "Hide in here." She and Tiffany dove into the nearest zippered compartment of the backpack.

"It's kind of stuffy in here," said Tiffany, squirming to find a comfortable position.

"I know, but we can't let anyone see us. Besides, there's nothing else in this pocket. No rocks or chewed-up pencils. We have the place to ourselves."

"That's true," said Tiffany.

And so the dolls settled in to wait for Kate to take them home.

CHAPTER SIX

A True Menace

ANNABELLE and Tiffany waited impatiently in the backpack for the last bell of the day to ring. When it did, Annabelle said, "Yay!" and Tiffany said, "Finally."

A few minutes later, over the noise in the hall, the dolls heard Kate say, "Call me tonight, Ayanna," and then, "Hey, wait up!"

The backpack was grabbed off the shelf, and the dolls were jerked from side to side as a pair of arms slipped into it. And then, at last, they were being bumped along through the halls of the school. Annabelle could tell when they were outside again. The darkness in the pocket lightened slightly, and the roar of voices died away.

The walk home was quieter than Annabelle had thought it would be. She had distinctly heard Kate tell someone to wait up, but now she heard no voices. She wanted to ask Tiffany about this, but she dared not make a sound. Presently, and in fact sooner than Annabelle had expected, she heard a door being opened and closed.

And then, "Hello, is that you?"

"Yup, it's me. Are there any cookies?"

"In the cabinet."

A little girl's voice said, "Don't hog those!"

Nora's voice? wondered Annabelle. It didn't sound exactly like Nora's. And she thought one of the other voices sounded like it might belong to a boy. Had Kate invited a boy over? Annabelle didn't think Kate had any friends who were boys.

For the next hour Annabelle and Tiffany sat silently in the backpack, listening to the voices and sounds around them. Annabelle held Tiffany's hand, because she was growing nervous. Something was wrong. The voices were wrong, the sounds were wrong, even the names were wrong—BJ and Callie. And Mom, which was wrong too, because Mrs. Palmer didn't come home from work until almost suppertime. The only grown-up who should be at home was Grandma Katherine.

Without warning, the backpack was lifted off the ground and carried somewhere (up a flight of stairs, Annabelle thought), then set down. The voices shifted and moved away. Downstairs, maybe. Annabelle heard thumps and the voices calling to one another and doors opening and closing nearby and finally, further away, car doors opening and closing. Eventually she heard the car's engine start up and roar to life, then grow fainter.

The house was in silence.

"Where do you think we are?" whispered Tiffany.

"I don't know, but I have a feeling we're not in Kate's room."

The dolls remained in the backpack until

they guessed that half an hour had passed. They did not hear a sound.

"Do you think it's safe to look out?" Annabelle asked.

Tiffany nodded, and she and Annabelle stood up and peeked into the room.

Annabelle's eyes widened. She swallowed hard.

Next to her Tiffany whispered, "Uh-oh. I think we're in the wrong house."

Annabelle remembered the day before when she had sat on the shelf above Kate's coat, looking down at the floor, and had thought she was the most scared she had ever been. She realized that whatever she had felt then was nothing compared to what she felt now as she gazed around the room she and Tiffany were in and realized that Tiffany was right—this was not a room in the Palmers' house. She and Tiffany had explored the Palmers' house much too thoroughly to have missed something like this. No, this was a bedroom she had never seen before. And Annabelle was pretty sure it was a boy's bedroom.

"Tiffany," said Annabelle, "we're in the

wrong house, and it's Friday night. We won't even be able to try to get back to school until Monday. We will have been away from home for four days. Our parents were probably panicking when we didn't come back last night. They must have been hoping and hoping we'd come back tonight. Now we won't be able to get home until Monday, and we might not even get home then. What if whoever this backpack belongs to doesn't take it to school on Monday? What then? What if someone sticks the backpack in a closet and forgets about it and—"

"Annabelle! For heaven's sake. Stop saying things like that. Let's wait and see what happens on Monday. If we can't go back to school in a backpack, we'll go in a lunchbox or something. I'm not going to worry about that now. Let's just try to get through the weekend."

"I'd give anything to be stuck up in that soap dish again while Nora plays Miami Beach-a-go-go," said Annabelle. "How did we get in the wrong backpack, anyway?"

"The scarf must have been moved," replied Tiffany. "I bet it got shoved aside, and we climbed up the coat that was next to Kate's. We heard her voice in the hall, remember? So she was nearby."

Annabelle sighed. She gazed around the room. "Look at this mess," she said.

Annabelle had never seen a bedroom with so much stuff in it. Even Nora's messy room was tidier than this one. The floor here

was an ocean of paper scraps and glue bottles, crumbs and empty pretzel bags, plastic lizards and dinosaurs, Lego pieces, cardboard tubes from paper-towel rolls, seashells, tiny metal trucks, and open paperback books. Spilling from the shelves were magazines and banks and coins and markers and pencils and cassettes and baseballs, and boxes with padlocks,

and drawings of cars and spaceships
and aliens. Covering the walls were
more drawings and several posters of
baseball players. The door to the
room was open, and Annabelle
could see three handwritten
signs on it. One said MY ROOM.
One said DO NOT ENTAR. One
said BOY'S ONLY. On a table next
to the bed was a glass tank containing
four goldfish. And on the floor under
a window was a bigger glass tank, this
one holding an enormous lizard.

When Annabelle saw the lizard
she nearly screamed, but she caught
herself in time. "Tiffany!" she whispered loudly. "Look!"

"I know," said Tiffany,
following Annabelle's
gaze. "I wonder what
kind of lizard it is."

"Probably the kind that eats dolls," Annabelle muttered.

"Oh, Annabelle," said Tiffany. She paused. "What's that sound?"

"What sound?"

"Shh. Be quiet and listen for a minute."

Annabelle held herself very still. She heard the faraway hum of a refrigerator, and the whoosh of a car outside.

And then from very nearby—*chirp, chirp, chirp.*

Annabelle glanced at Tiffany, and Tiffany raised her eyebrows.

Chirp, chirp, chirp.

Tiffany was gazing around the room. "Hey, there's a whole cage full of crickets next to the lizard," she said.

"Oh, *ew!*" cried Annabelle as her eyes settled on the crickets. "Poor things. You know what they're for, don't you, Tiffany?"

"No. What?"

"They're the lizard's food."

"The lizard eats crickets?"

"Alive," said Annabelle emphatically.

"That's disgusting."

"Well, at least we don't have to worry that it'll eat us."

Annabelle and Tiffany watched the lizard and the crickets for a while. Still they heard no human voices and no sound of humans. "I think we could get out of the backpack," said Annabelle. "Don't you?"

"I guess so," replied Tiffany. "We can't get into much more trouble than we're already in."

Annabelle, thinking of Doll State, said nothing, but climbed out of the backpack. Since the backpack had been set on the floor, she and Tiffany were out in the messy room in no time. They began to wade through the papers and crumbs and trucks and dinosaurs.

"Aughh!" screamed Annabelle as she came face to face with a lizard that was exactly as tall as she was.

"Relax, it's plastic," said Tiffany.

Annabelle grabbed Tiffany's hand and clutched it as they continued across the room. They were approaching several metal racing cars that Tiffany hoped she could fit in when, out of the corner of her eye, Annabelle saw something move. She whirled around in time to see two dolls, a small one followed by an absolutely enormous one, enter the room.

Annabelle tugged on Tiffany's hand, pointed to the dolls, put her finger to her lips, and pulled Tiffany behind a hill of wadded-up papers. Cautiously, she and Tiffany peered around the hill. Annabelle saw that the small doll, who was taller than Annabelle, but still much smaller than the other doll, was dressed as a princess. She wore a glittery lavender dress, and lavender slippers with silk ribbons that twined and criss-crossed up her legs. On her head sat a lavender crown studded with plastic rubies and emeralds. And in her hand was a wand topped by a sparkling star.

The large doll was, Annabelle guessed, almost as tall as Nora, and she was wearing a short dress and a pair of shoes that Annabelle was pretty sure would fit Nora just fine. She lurched after the princess doll, crashing stiffly along, since her arms and legs were jointed only at the shoulders and hips, and she couldn't bend her elbows or knees.

"*What on earth—*" Tiffany started to whisper to Annabelle, as she glared at the giant doll.

At that moment the princess turned to face the giant and commanded, "Charge!"

Annabelle completely forgot about being quiet. "How do they even know we're here?" she squeaked to Tiffany.

But Tiffany nudged her, shaking her head, and Annabelle saw the princess point not at them, but across the room. As she watched, the giant lurched forward, nearly smashing into a group of small dolls huddled beneath a table. The dolls screamed and scattered, looking, Annabelle thought, for better hiding places.

"After them!" the princess shouted.

The giant changed direction and stomped after the fleeing dolls.

Annabelle and Tiffany locked eyes. They didn't need to speak to know what they must do. They leapt to their feet and ran from behind the hill of papers.

Tiffany raised her arm. "We'll help you!" she cried. "Go hide in that backpack."

One of the dolls, who was Annabelle's size and wearing yellow pajamas and a pair of fuzzy yellow slippers, replied, "There are too many of us. We don't have enough time." She glanced wildly around the room. "Quick. In there!"

"Us, too?" asked Tiffany.

"Yes, hurry."

Annabelle and Tiffany followed the dolls through the low doorway of a strange structure. And Annabelle, peeping through a narrow window, saw the giant's shoe smash down on the spot where she had just been standing.

CHAPTER SEVEN

The Longest Night

WHO—WHO ARE you?" asked the doll in the yellow slippers.

Annabelle turned away from the window. The building in which she now found herself was a hut, made of small plastic blocks. Lego, she realized. Probably built by the boy whose room this was.

"Yeah, who are you?" shouted a voice from outside.

"That's Mean Mimi," whispered the doll in the slippers.

Annabelle and Tiffany peered through the window again and saw the princess doll standing only a few inches away, hands on hips.

Tiffany poked her head out the window. "I'm Tiffany Funcraft and this is my best friend, Annabelle Doll," she called.

"What are you doing here?" asked Mean Mimi.

"Don't answer," hissed the doll in the slippers. "It's better not to talk to her."

Tiffany pulled her head inside, and Annabelle watched Mean Mimi wait a moment for an answer, then call to the giant, "Come on, Sandra. Leave them alone for now." The princess and the giant left the room, and the princess slammed the door shut behind her. Annabelle was facing the oddest assortment of dolls that she'd seen since her days,

89

more than a hundred years ago, in the old doll maker's workshop in London. The doll in the yellow slippers was standing between two other dolls, one wearing pink pajamas and pink fuzzy slippers, and the other wearing blue pajamas and blue fuzzy slippers. Their hair and skin color were different, Annabelle noted, but otherwise their faces looked just alike. Next to the pajama dolls were two . . . what? Annabelle had seen dolls like them somewhere before, she thought. And then she remembered the day Kate had come home from school with a doll lent to her by Rachel.

It was chubby and squat with a wild frizz of brilliantly colored hair, which Kate had spent nearly an hour braiding and unbraiding and braiding again. What had Kate called the

doll? A troll, Annabelle thought. And now here were two trolls next to the dolls in pajamas. Each was wearing a sort of poncho made of a scrap of fabric with a hole cut in the center, which had been slipped over her head. One troll's hair was bright blue, and the other's was a rainbow of colors.

Annabelle was so fascinated by the troll dolls that at first she didn't see the six other dolls in the hut. When she did, she let out a gasp. These dolls were behind the trolls, and . . . they looked as though they were floating. Then Annabelle realized that only five appeared to float. The sixth was holding on to a yellow Lego above the doorway. The others fluttered and flapped below her on a draft of air. The dolls were made of paper, pale green paper, and they hung in a wavering line, joined at their hands.

The doll in the yellow slippers stepped forward. "Where did you—I mean, do you live here?" she asked.

"No," said Annabelle. "We're here by mistake. We live at Kate Palmer's house, and we accidentally got in her backpack before she went to school yesterday, and then we got out of her backpack in school so we could see what school is like, and then we climbed in the wrong backpack, not Kate's. . . ." Annabelle trailed off.

"And when we got out of that backpack," Tiffany spoke up, "we were here." She paused. "Where are we, anyway?"

"This is BJ's room."

"Is BJ a boy?"

One of the trolls stepped forward. "Yup. BJ Gordon."

Tiffany looked at Annabelle. "BJ Gordon. Is he in Kate's class?"

"I'm not sure," replied Annabelle, frowning. "Are you BJ's dolls?" she asked.

The blue-haired troll laughed. "No, we belong to Callie."

"Callie? Who's Callie?" asked Tiffany.

"She's BJ's sister. Her room is next door. We come in here to hide sometimes."

"What are your names?" Annabelle asked timidly.

The doll in the yellow slippers put her arms around the other dolls in slippers and said, "We're the PJ Party Pals. I'm Yvonne, that's Penny in the pink, and that's Beth in the blue. And these," she continued, "are the Troll Twins. Callie didn't give them names, and they didn't come with names, so they named themselves."

"I'm Waterfall," said the troll with the blue hair. "Isn't that the most beautiful name you've ever heard?"

"And I'm Magnificent Mariah Raynebow," said the other troll. "But you can call me Melody for short."

The chain of paper dolls fluttered as Waterfall walked by them. "We're the Cutouts," they said in unison.

Annabelle looked at the outline of their green dresses and hair, at their plain, featureless faces, and waited to hear their names. But they said nothing more, just swayed gently on an air current.

"You come in here to hide," Tiffany repeated. "From Callie?"

"No, from Mean Mimi," said Waterfall.

"But who is Mean Mimi?" asked Annabelle. "And why does she want that giant doll to chase after you?"

Melody sighed. "Let's sit down," she said. "It's kind of a long story."

"A long story," echoed the Cutouts.

Annabelle and Tiffany sat on the floor in the center of the Lego hut with the PJ Party Pals and the Troll Twins. The Cutouts swayed near the doorway.

"Mean Mimi's real name," began Melody, "is Princess Mimi. She arrived two years ago. The rest of us were already here. Callie likes dolls, and she has a lot of them. Most of us are alive."

"I'm usually the one to give the oath," said Waterfall proudly.

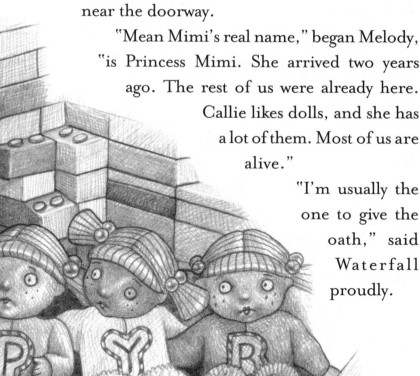

"Oh, yes, she gives the oath," said the Cutouts.

"Anyway, when Mimi first arrived," continued Melody, "we all wanted to be her friend. We thought she was beautiful. She was nice and funny and *she* seemed to want to be *our* friend."

"But soon," said Beth, "we saw how bossy she was. She was always telling us to do this and do that. Why? Because she thinks she's a *real* princess, not a doll in princess clothes."

"She thinks one day she's going to be Queen of All Dolls," added Penny. "*All* dolls, as in, all the dolls in the world."

"The Queen of All Dolls," sang the Cutouts.

"So she ordered us around," said Melody. "She expected us to do whatever she said. She told us to get things for her and do favors for her, so she could have everything she wanted. At first we didn't mind. We were just so happy that this beautiful girl, this girl who was so smart and confident and—and—"

"Exotic," said the Cutouts.

"Right, exotic," agreed Melody. "That

this wonderful, exotic girl wanted to be our friend. Each of us hoped to be her *best* friend. Then one by one we saw Mimi for what she was. A bully."

"We began calling her Mean Mimi instead of Princess Mimi," said Waterfall.

"We told her we weren't going to be her friends anymore," continued Melody. "We said she didn't know the true meaning of friendship."

Annabelle opened her eyes wide. "What did she say?"

"She said, 'You'll be sorry. You'll pay for this.' And she started doing all these mean things to us."

"Why didn't you just ignore her?" asked Tiffany.

"We tried to," said Yvonne. "In the beginning."

"In the beginning," chorused the Cut-outs.

"But there are other dolls here," said Melody, "and Mean Mimi has turned some of them against us. The ones she can control."

"You mean like the giant?" asked Annabelle.

"Yes," said Beth. "That's the Sandra doll. She's the most dangerous, I guess, since she's the biggest. There are others as well."

"Techno-Man and Sleeping Billy," whispered the Cutouts.

"Any others?" asked Tiffany.

"Nope. It's Mean Mimi, the Sandra doll, Techno-Man, and Sleeping Billy against the rest of us," said Waterfall.

"Who are Techno-Man and Sleeping Billy?" asked Annabelle, looking nervously out the window. "And," she went on, "how come we haven't heard the Sandra doll say anything? Does she talk?"

"Does she talk? Does she talk? No, she doesn't talk," sang the Cutouts.

Melody drew in a deep breath. "All right. Here's the deal. Like I said, Mean Mimi's friends—she calls them friends, but they aren't *true* friends—are the dolls she can control. Take the Sandra doll. She may be big, but she's really a baby, a baby who's just learned how to walk. We don't know exactly how Mean Mimi controls her, but we think the Sandra doll is afraid of her. And she's too young to know what to do about that. So she just does

whatever Mimi tells
her to do."

"Yeah, like go crash-
ing around and stepping
on us," said Beth.

"Then there's
Techno-Man," said
Melody. "He's
actually on Mimi's
side *voluntarily*."

"He should
know better,"
said the
Cutouts.

"And
he's . . ."
Melody paused
dramatically. "He's
an *action figure*," she
whispered.

"*What?*"
shrieked Annabelle.

"Action figures *never*
take the oath!" cried
Tiffany. She turned to
Annabelle in alarm.

Annabelle recalled a night, years earlier, when she had pestered Nanny with questions about the oath and Doll State and upholding the Doll Code of Honor. She distinctly remembered Nanny saying, "Oh, no. Action figures don't take the oath. They're too destructive. They would never agree to work for the benefit of dollkind. Even if one did agree, he would be in PDS in the blink of an eye. Action figures are out of control."

And now here was Melody saying, "We don't know what happened. One day Techno-Man just got up and walked out of a bucket of action figures."

"It was really scary," said Yvonne.

"Now we're afraid of the

whole bucket," added Penny.

Good lord, thought Annabelle. I'm certainly glad I don't live in this house. The Captain was beginning to seem friendly by comparison.

"What does Techno-Man do?" asked Tiffany.

"Oh, you'll probably see," replied Waterfall.

"Yes, you'll see," sang the Cutouts.

"He's got all these gadgets—rockets and lasers and stuff," said Melody.

"Do they work? Are they real?" asked Annabelle.

"Sort of," said Yvonne.

"Not really," said Beth.

"He's *very* scary," said Penny.

"What about Sleeping Billy?" asked Tiffany.

"Sleeping Billy," repeated Melody. "Well, Sleeping Billy is a real baby, much more of a baby than the Sandra doll."

"He's an infant," said Waterfall.

"He's bigger than Mean Mimi, though," said Penny. "He's even bigger than Techno-Man. He's this soft baby doll wearing a bunting with a hood. Only his plastic face peeks out of the bunting. And all he wants to do is play. With whatever you put in front of him. But he'll do what Mean Mimi tells him to do."

"The thing is," said Waterfall, "that his eyes can open and close. And they close every time he lies down. And whenever his eyes close he immediately falls asleep. So he's not much good to Mimi, except that because he's stuffed it's pretty hard for him to get hurt."

Annabelle once again peered out the window of the Lego hut. BJ's room seemed quiet. "Where do you suppose everybody is?" she asked. "I still don't see Mean Mimi. Or anybody."

"They're probably next door in Callie's room," replied Beth.

"In Mean Mimi's headquarters," chorused the Cutouts.

"That's where her throne and her robe are. All her princess stuff. She came with lots and lots of accessories," Waterfall explained.

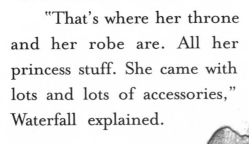

"But right now, I'm sure she's getting ready for an attack."

"An attack?" cried Annabelle. "On us? What if the humans see?"

"Oh, they won't see," said Melody.

"No, they never see," sang the Cutouts.

"They go away every weekend. We're on our own here until Sunday night." Melody made a face.

"What—what kind of attack?" asked Annabelle.

"Mean Mimi plans all sorts of things," said Penny. "Usually she sets up BJ's racetrack with one end—the high end—in Callie's room, and the low end in here. Then she launches racing cars at us like missiles. She does other things too, of course. She attaches all of Techno-Man's gadgets to him and sends him after us. And she sets the Sandra doll on us. Whatever she can think of."

"That's how mad she is that we aren't her friends anymore," Melody concluded.

The dolls were silent for a few moments. Then the Cutouts dropped to the floor and glided by a window, each peering outside in turn. The PJ Party Pals and the Troll Twins began testing the sides of the Lego hut, wondering how sturdy it was.

Annabelle pulled Tiffany away from the others. "We're stuck here until Sunday," she whispered.

Tiffany nodded. "So we'll have to help out in the fight against Mean Mimi. It's the only thing to do."

Annabelle pressed her lips together and blinked her eyes. "I know," she said at last.

CHAPTER EIGHT

Spies

ANNABELLE, feeling shaky but determined, took Tiffany's hand and led her back to the center of the hut where the PJ Party Pals and the Troll Twins were now standing in a small knot, talking quietly. "We've had a discussion, and we've decided to help you in your fight this weekend," she said firmly. "On Monday, we'll have to try to get back home. But until then, we want to help."

"Thank you," said Penny. "That's really nice of you. But this isn't going to be easy, you know. In fact, it's dangerous. A few of us have gotten broken. So if you want to hide or something, you can. We won't mind."

"We're used to this," added Waterfall, heaving a great sigh.

Annabelle looked down at her china arms and legs, at her petticoat and lace and ruffles. If she got hurt in the fight and went home to Kate cracked or smashed or with her clothing ripped or even missing, Kate might be suspicious, and Annabelle would go into Doll State. Or would she? Annabelle thought about the Doll Code of Honor. A living doll, she reminded herself, was bound to protect the secret life of dolls. But a living doll was also bound to work for the benefit of dollkind. And what could be more beneficial to dollkind than preventing a cruel princess from trying to take away the freedom that living dolls now enjoyed? Annabelle wasn't sure (and she wished very hard that she could talk to Mama or Papa about this), but she thought that perhaps it would be okay to risk herself and Kate's suspicions if, in the end, all dollkind would benefit.

So now she said bravely to Yvonne, "No, we want to help you. What do we do first?"

"Well, the walls here seem sturdy enough. I think this can be our hideout, at least for a while."

"We don't want it to get smashed, though," said Melody. "We'd never be able to put it put back together before BJ comes home. So if Mimi is planning something really big, we'll have to abandon it."

"The Cutouts are going to go on a spy mission," spoke up Beth, "to see if they can figure out what Mimi is up to."

Annabelle looked at the Cutouts and nudged Tiffany. The Cutouts were busily fastening on their spy outfits—paper hats and sunglasses. The hats were identical—yellow sombreros—except for the one worn by the doll at one end of the line. Her sombrero was red. When they were dressed, they took turns peering out a window as they glided by it.

"We'll be back," said the doll in

the red hat as she opened the door. Annabelle guessed she was the head Cutout.

"In no time," chorused the others.

Annabelle and Tiffany watched as the Cutouts slipped across BJ's room to the wall nearest the door. They moved smoothly, following the orders of the doll in the red hat.

"Up!" she would call, as she climbed nimbly up a bookcase or a stack of toys, the rest of the Cutouts behind her.

"Down," she would cry, and the Cutouts would change direction.

"Around. Careful. Crack the whip!"

The Cutouts circled BJ's room, peering into corners and under pieces of furniture. Eventually, they returned to the Lego hut.

"No one's in here," reported the head Cutout.

"No one at all," said the others.

"So we're off to Callie's room."

"Keep your wits about you," said Waterfall gravely.

"Our wits, our wits," sang the Cutouts, and the next thing Annabelle knew, they had

slithered under the closed door and disappeared into the hallway.

Fifteen minutes later they returned. They zipped into the hut in a great rush. Annabelle thought they were quivering.

"What did you see?" asked Penny.

"Oh, it's horrible, it's awful, it's a crime and a disaster," cried the Cutouts.

"What? What?" said Tiffany.

The news was distressing. Mean Mimi was, in fact, building a racetrack between Callie's room and BJ's. She had ordered Sleeping Billy to line up Callie's metal cars and trucks by the head of the track.

"She'll probably make Techno-Man launch them," said Beth.

Techno-Man, the Cutouts reported, was checking his lasers and spinning his gadgets and looking important.

"What about the Sandra doll?" asked Yvonne.

"Just sitting on her blanket," replied the head Cutout.

"Waiting for her orders," added the others.

Melody sighed. "It'll be an all-out attack," she said. "I'm sure of it. Mean Mimi is angry."

"Angrier than usual," said Waterfall.

"Why?" asked Annabelle.

"Because last night she stomped in here—"

"While BJ was right in his bed!" exclaimed Penny.

"—and demanded to know why we won't be her friends. And we told her—"

"Like we've told her about a thousand times," said Beth.

"—that she's not going to have *true* friends until she stops being so mean and bossy and wanting to take over the world."

"I said," added Melody, "that the Sandra doll and the others only stick with her because they're afraid of her, not because they actually like her. She's just a big bully, and bullies don't have real friends, only underlings."

"She's fit to be tied," sang the Cutouts.

"What should we do?" asked Tiffany.

"We have to prepare for the attack," said Yvonne.

"We know what to do," said Waterfall, sounding resigned.

"Unfortunately, we can't always prevent damage," said Melody.

Annabelle, who had been sitting on the floor next to Tiffany, stood up. "What I want to know," she said boldly, "is how Mean Mimi can keep getting away with this. If BJ and his family come home after their weekends away and find messes or broken dolls or smashed Lego buildings, then the Doll Code of Honor has been broken, and someone should go into Doll State. Mimi is putting all dolls at risk with her attacks."

"That's true," agreed Beth. "The thing is, so far no one has actually caught her in the act. But we think it's just a matter of time before something so big, so absolutely horrendous happens that . . . that . . . well, maybe all of us here will go into Doll State."

"Or even Permanent Doll State," said Melody.

Annabelle's hand flew to her mouth, and she gasped. She wanted to ask these new dolls if they really believed in PDS, but now wasn't the time.

"We don't know how to stop Mean Mimi, though," said Penny. "At least not yet. We talk to her, but she doesn't listen to us. And we can't overpower her while she controls Techno-Man and Sleeping Billy and the Sandra doll. So all we can do is ward off her attacks."

"And we'd better be prepared," said Melody. "Come on, everybody. Let's get to work. Beth, you're in charge of barricades. Waterfall, you're in charge of booby traps. Cutouts, plan your next spy mission."

"Okay," replied Beth. "Melody, you and Tiffany will work with me."

"That leaves Annabelle, Yvonne, and Penny to work with me," said Waterfall.

"Off we go, off we go," sang the Cutouts, donning their hats and glasses and once again gliding toward BJ's door.

And so the preparations began. Annabelle and her group set traps around the room.

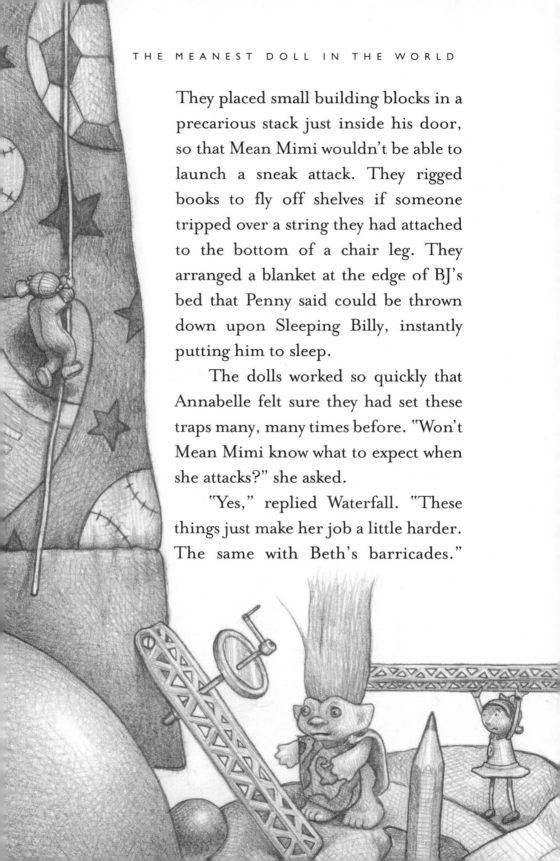

They placed small building blocks in a precarious stack just inside his door, so that Mean Mimi wouldn't be able to launch a sneak attack. They rigged books to fly off shelves if someone tripped over a string they had attached to the bottom of a chair leg. They arranged a blanket at the edge of BJ's bed that Penny said could be thrown down upon Sleeping Billy, instantly putting him to sleep.

The dolls worked so quickly that Annabelle felt sure they had set these traps many, many times before. "Won't Mean Mimi know what to expect when she attacks?" she asked.

"Yes," replied Waterfall. "These things just make her job a little harder. The same with Beth's barricades."

Annabelle eyed the piles of toys and pieces from BJ's erector set. "They won't do much except delay the worst of the damage. Sometimes Sleeping Billy and the Sandra doll get tired and want to go back to Callie's room before things are totally out of control. It's the most we can hope for."

It was very late at night when the last of the barricades was in place, and the last of the booby traps had been set.

Annabelle, Tiffany, the Troll Twins, and the PJ Party Pals returned to the Lego hut.

"What did you see?" Melody asked as the Cutouts returned from another spy mission.

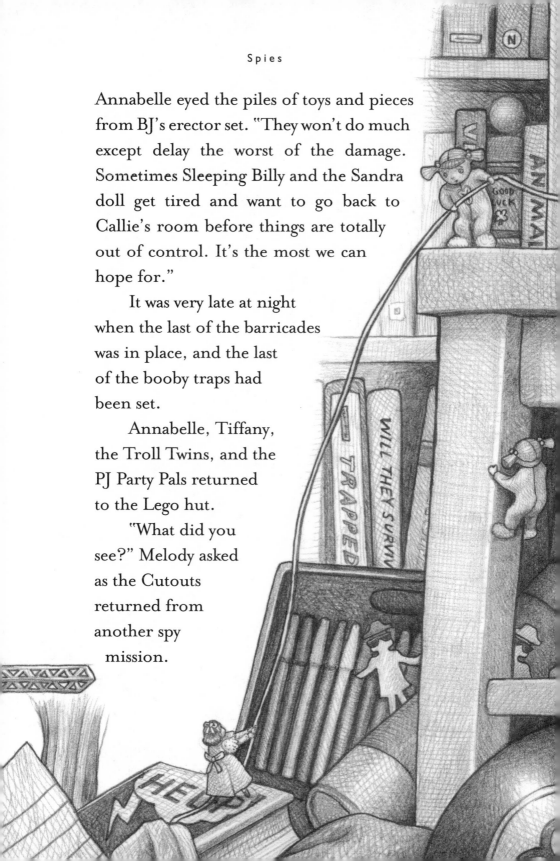

"Eleven o'clock and all's well," sang the head Cutout.

"All's well, all's well," chorused the others.

Annabelle and Tiffany looked at each other and shrugged. "I guess Mean Mimi is planning a surprise attack," said Tiffany.

"It won't be too much of a surprise. Mimi will knock over a booby trap as soon as she comes in the room," replied Annabelle.

The dolls huddled in the Lego hut and waited.

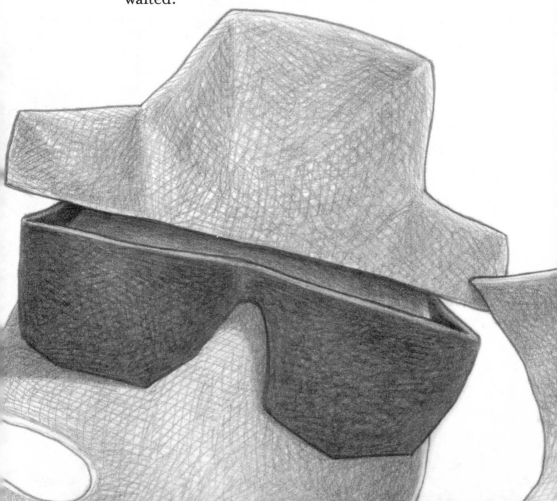

They waited throughout the night. They waited all the next morning.

"If we wait much longer, BJ and his family will come home and see our traps and barricades," said Tiffany.

"Maybe that's what Mean Mimi hopes will happen," Annabelle whispered to her. "She's just bluffing. She'll get us in trouble without even—"

Z Z Z Z Z Z Z.

A low buzz sounded from the hallway outside BJ's room.

Annabelle jumped.

The buzz grew louder and louder.

"What is it?" cried Tiffany.

"Techno-Man!" shrieked Penny.

The buzzing was drowned out then by the crash of the pile of building blocks as the door to BJ's room burst open.

Annabelle peeped through the window of the hut and saw the end of the race-track poised in the doorway. A small metal ambulance came hurtling down the track, sailed through the air, and crashed against the hut.

Annabelle jerked back from the window.

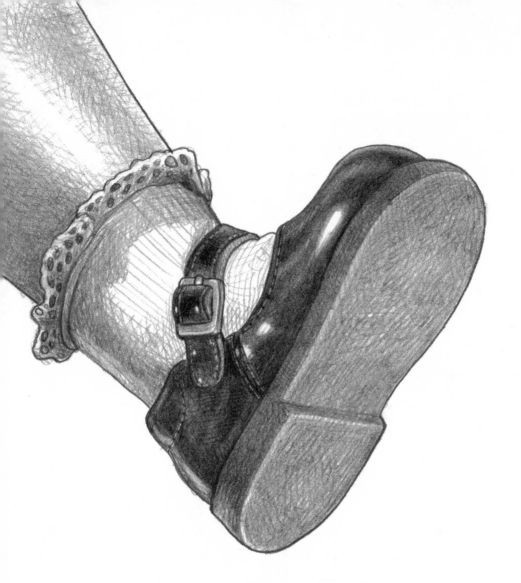

 But not before she saw a giant foot stride into the room. The Sandra doll was back. And she was not alone.

"Honey, I'm home!" called Mean Mimi.

CHAPTER NINE

Chaos

MEAN MIMI, resplendent in her princess garb, ran into the room alongside the Sandra doll.

"Get that!" she cried, pointing to a pile of toys.

The Sandra doll kicked the toys, sending them crashing to the floor.

"And that!" Mean Mimi cried.

This time the Sandra doll kicked through one of Beth's barricades.

"What if she kicks the hut?" asked Annabelle in a quavering voice.

Melody looked at the walls of the hut in

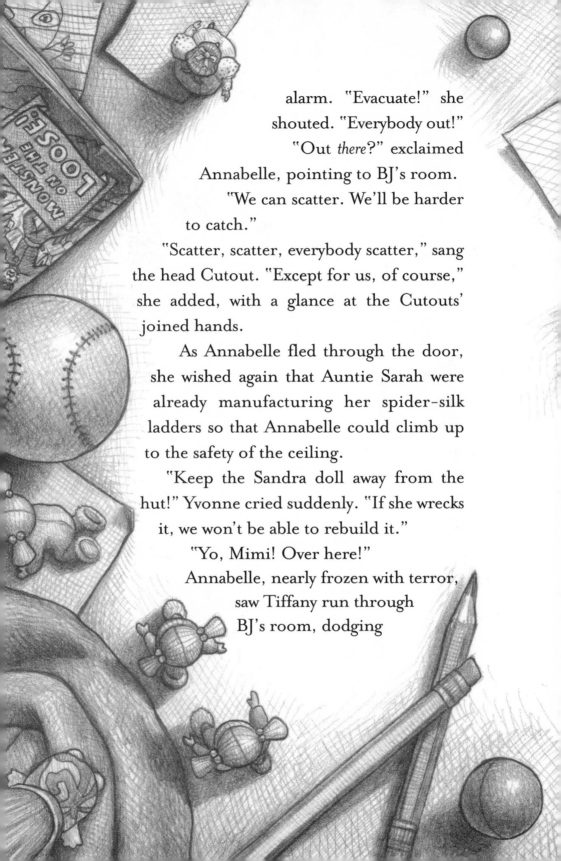

alarm. "Evacuate!" she shouted. "Everybody out!"

"Out *there*?" exclaimed Annabelle, pointing to BJ's room.

"We can scatter. We'll be harder to catch."

"Scatter, scatter, everybody scatter," sang the head Cutout. "Except for us, of course," she added, with a glance at the Cutouts' joined hands.

As Annabelle fled through the door, she wished again that Auntie Sarah were already manufacturing her spider-silk ladders so that Annabelle could climb up to the safety of the ceiling.

"Keep the Sandra doll away from the hut!" Yvonne cried suddenly. "If she wrecks it, we won't be able to rebuild it."

"Yo, Mimi! Over here!"

Annabelle, nearly frozen with terror, saw Tiffany run through BJ's room, dodging

booby traps and piles of toys. She
reached a far corner, stuck her
thumbs in her ears, and wiggled
her fingers at Mean Mimi.
"Nyah, nyah-nyah, nyah,
nyah!" she called, which
was something Annabelle
had always wanted to do.

Mean Mimi turned and
saw Tiffany. "Go get her!"
she ordered the Sandra doll.

The Sandra doll
hesitated. She looked
pleadingly at Mimi.

FEAR·

"Oh, all right," said Mimi, sounding highly annoyed. She grabbed a large blanket that had been lying nearby and heaved it toward the Sandra doll. The Sandra doll, big but clumsy as a toddler, tried to catch the blanket, missed it, lurched forward a few steps, then bent to pick it up. She draped it around her neck and stuck her thumb in her mouth. Then she lumbered across the room in the direction of Tiffany.

Mean Mimi turned her attention to Sleeping Billy, who was sitting on the floor amid BJ's toys, picking them up, dropping them, patting them, putting them in his mouth. "On your feet, you big baby!" she ordered him, and she grabbed his hand and tugged at him. "You're supposed to be helping us," said Mean Mimi, puffing. "Catch somebody, break something, get going!"

Sleeping Billy tottered after the Sandra doll.

Annabelle looked around BJ's room and was just think-ing that the attack wasn't as bad as she had thought it would be—certainly it was not moving along very quickly—when she heard a great clinking and clanking from the hallway, and turned around to see two things happen at once. First a bar-rage of metal cars and trucks began sailing off the end of the racetrack and soaring through BJ's room. And then, with the missiles still flying, a man dressed in a suit that appeared to be composed almost entirely of gadgets, an important-looking helmet on his head, strode grimly through the doorway. He was carrying what looked to Annabelle like a laser stick in one hand. Nearly as frightening were the blinking lights on his helmet.

Annabelle couldn't help herself. She let out a scream, and for a few seconds every-one in BJ's room stopped what she or he was doing. And in those quiet seconds Annabelle realized that the fighting man's helmet wasn't just blinking, it was making all

sorts of noises—beeping and bleeping and pinging and buzzing and zapping.

Annabelle hid her eyes, and suddenly . . . chaos.

Annabelle opened her eyes in time to see the missiles begin to land in the room. They knocked toys off BJ's bookshelves. They smashed into the drawings tacked to the wall, and one ripped the corner off a baseball poster. Another put a nick in the headboard of the bed. One slammed into Yvonne and knocked her off her feet. One popped the top off the lizard's cage. And one soared toward Tiffany.

"Duck!" shrieked Annabelle, and Tiffany dropped to the ground as a fire truck shot toward her head.

Moments later a Jeep landed in the

middle of the room and skidded into Mean Mimi, causing her to fall backward and land on her bottom. Annabelle would have laughed if she hadn't been so frightened.

"Calm, calm, everybody calm," Annabelle heard the Cutouts sing.

"Oh, shut up," said Mean Mimi.

"Jealous, she's jealous, always jealous," was the reply.

"Sandra, Sleeping Billy, Techno-Man!" cried Mean Mimi. "Doesn't anybody remember what we talked about?"

Sleeping Billy made his way across the room to the Sandra doll then, who took his hand.

"That's right. Teamwork!" said Mean Mimi.

The Sandra doll and Sleeping Billy turned woodenly and began marching through the room, not bothering to step over anything in their way. They trod on plastic animals and kicked through the rest of the barricades. They narrowly missed trampling Beth, who was helping Yvonne to her feet. And then Annabelle saw that they were headed for the Lego hut.

"Tiffany!" called Annabelle. "Help!"

Tiffany started across the room, but was stopped by Techno-Man. He stepped in front of her, feet planted solidly apart, holding his weapon in both hands. "Not one more step, missy, or I'll blast you," he said.

Tiffany looked at the beeping helmet. She looked at the laser. Then she looked Techno-Man in his eyes and said, "Okay. Go ahead."

There are so many advantages to being plastic, thought Annabelle.

Techno-Man glanced at Mean Mimi, who glared at him until he said, "Oh," as if he had just remembered something, and turned and ran out of the room.

As soon as he was gone, Tiffany continued in the direction of the Lego hut. She moved much faster than the Sandra doll and Sleeping Billy, and she reached it several seconds before they did. Then she stood by the doorway to the hut, put her hands on her hips, and sang, "Ta-ra-ra-boom-de-ay! I lost my pants today. I found them yesterday. Ta-ra-ra-BOOM-de-ay!"

Annabelle's mouth dropped open, and so did Mean Mimi's. But the PJ Party Pals, the Troll Twins, and even the Cutouts began to laugh. And then so did the Sandra doll and Sleeping Billy.

"Shut up!" Mean Mimi said furiously, but only the Sandra doll obeyed her.

Mean Mimi ran from the room.

As soon as she was out of sight, the Sandra doll began to laugh again.

But all the laughter stopped abruptly when there was another commotion in the hallway outside BJ's room, and then something happened so fast that later Annabelle had trouble describing it, even though she had seen it with her own eyes.

127

From the hallway Annabelle heard the
rumble of a motor, and the honking of a
toy car. And then a large pink VW Beetle
zoomed into the room, with Techno-Man
in the driver's seat, his helmet beeping and
ringing. Behind the car ran Mean Mimi, holding a complicated-looking box, with which,
Annabelle realized, she was controlling the
car. The car bumped over everything in its
path. It crunched over toys and markers and
papers. It knocked Sleeping Billy to the
ground, and he fell asleep in an instant. Just
when Annabelle was sure Mean Mimi was
going to crash the car into the hut, Techno-
Man leaped out of the driver's seat and
snatched up Penny.

"Gotcha!" he cried.

"Help!" yelped
Penny.

"After them!" shouted Melody, and she and Tiffany and Yvonne and Beth and Waterfall and even Annabelle began to chase the car.

They might actually have caught up with it, Annabelle thought, but in the confusion, Mimi steered the car into the lizard's cage, Penny escaped, and Techno-Man lost his helmet.

As the helmet tumbled to the ground Annabelle gasped. The beeping and pinging stopped, and Annabelle saw that Techno-Man wasn't an action figure after all. He was an ordinary boy doll wearing a fancy costume. His weapon was a toy; his helmet did nothing but make noise.

"Look, Tiffany!" exclaimed Annabelle. "He's just—"

"I know," replied Tiffany. "That's why I

told him to go ahead and blast me. I didn't think he could do it."

"Troops!" shouted Mean Mimi. "Assemble!"

Annabelle looked at Sleeping Billy nap–

ping on the floor; at Techno-Man, patting at his crew cut; at the Sandra doll, who was still giggling over Tiffany's song.

"I said, assemble!" Mimi hurried across the room to the Sandra doll and snatched away her blanket. "Come. HERE."

The Sandra doll whimpered, but turned to follow Mean Mimi.

And Annabelle, her eyes large, suddenly whispered something to Tiffany, who repeated it to Penny, Yvonne, and Beth. In a flash, Tiffany and the PJ Party Pals had ambushed Mimi and stolen the Sandra doll's blanket.

"*Now* try telling her what to do," Melody said to Mimi. "Order the Sandra doll around."

"Get over here, Sandra," Mean Mimi said weakly.

But the Sandra doll only gazed longingly at her blanket, which the PJ Party Pals were holding.

"She wants her blankie," Annabelle said, surprising herself. "She won't do anything you tell her to do unless you hand her the blankie, will she, Mimi? You can't control her."

"Oh no you can't, oh no you can't, oh no you can't control her," sang the Cutouts.

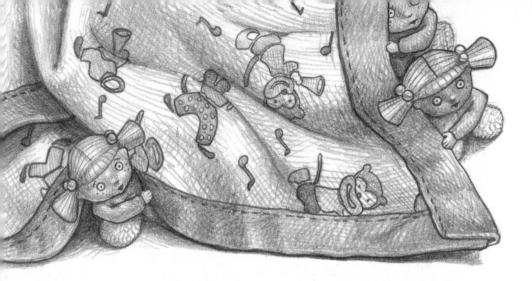

"All you have to do," Annabelle said to the PJ Party Pals, the Troll Twins, and the Cutouts, "is let the Sandra doll have her blankie—and be nice to her. She'll listen to you."

"Well . . . well . . . Techno-Man—" Mean Mimi began to splutter.

"You can't control him either," said Annabelle. "You never could. Techno-Man likes to show off. But he's not really an action figure. So nobody has any reason to be afraid of him."

"Get back here, Techno-Man!" Mean Mimi shouted. But Techno-Man was slinking through the door into the hallway. He gave a small wave over his shoulder and disappeared.

"Sleeping Billy will still do whatever I tell him," said Mimi.

Everyone looked across the room to

where Sleeping Billy lay in a bed of toys. The Sandra doll was sitting next to him, trying to cover him with her blanket.

"I have a feeling," said Annabelle quietly, "that Sleeping Billy just wants to be with the Sandra doll."

"Nice army," said Waterfall to Mimi.

Mean Mimi began to flounce out of the room. She was only halfway across it when Yvonne shrieked, "Oh, no!" and the Cutouts sang, "Beware the lizard!"

That was when Annabelle saw BJ's lizard slither over the top of his cage and disappear

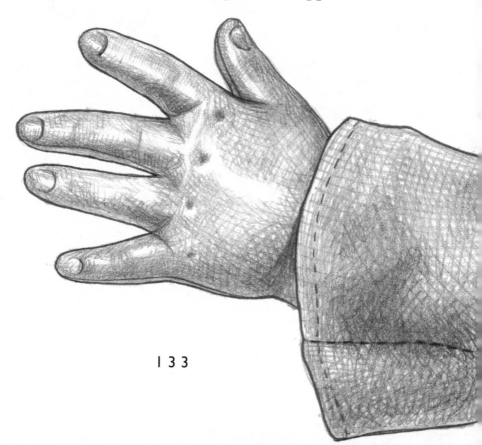

into the chaos of the room.
Screaming and hollering,
Annabelle, Tiffany, and their
new friends ran for the Lego
hut, and Mean Mimi fled into
the hallway, leaving the Sandra
doll and Sleeping Billy behind.
Annabelle watched the Sandra doll
tug at Sleeping Billy and help him
out of the room.

All was quiet at last,
except for the sound of
many crickets chirping.

CHAPTER TEN

Order

THE DOLLS HID in the Lego hut for two hours. They huddled in the middle, as far from the door as possible, even though Annabelle pointed out that the lizard probably didn't know how to open doors. Finally Melody said, "You know we're going to have to go out there and find Carl. Carl is the lizard," she told Annabelle and Tiffany. "We have to clean up the mess too. We can't leave BJ's room looking like this."

The other dolls nodded.

"What are we going to do with Carl when we find him?" asked Tiffany.

"Get him back in his cage somehow," said Melody.

Annabelle was barely listening to this conversation. A very worrisome thought had occurred to her. Finally she asked, "Does BJ's room get this messy every weekend?"

"Usually," replied Penny. "Sometimes even messier."

"Messier," whispered the Cutouts.

"Do you always manage to put everything back in order before BJ's family comes home?"

"We try. BJ's room is so messy that it's a little hard to tell," said Yvonne. "We figure he won't notice if a few things aren't just as he left them."

"Has there ever been anything big that you couldn't fix?" asked Annabelle. "I mean, did you ever have to leave a Lego building broken, or Carl loose, or something heavy knocked over?"

Melody stared at Annabelle. "Why?" she asked. "What are you trying to say?"

"Well, I'm just looking around at this mess"—Annabelle pointed out the window of the Lego hut—"and thinking how hard it will be to clean up. And I'm wondering what will happen if we can't catch Carl. I *know* we can't fix the rip in that poster, or the nick on the bed. And I'm guessing this happens almost every weekend—that there's some little something still broken or torn or out of place when BJ comes home." Annabelle paused and drew in a breath. "Don't you think maybe BJ's family is starting to get suspicious?" she said finally.

Before anybody spoke, Annabelle had her answer. The faces of the other dolls told her everything. And Annabelle felt something inside of her grow very heavy.

After a moment Waterfall sighed and said, "We do think they're getting suspicious."

"And what," went on Annabelle, wishing she didn't have to say this, "do you think that is going to mean for other dolls in other humans' houses?"

"We don't know," said Melody. "We can barely stand to think about it. We just clean up here as well as we can and hope for the best."

"Mean Mimi," said Annabelle slowly, "is a menace to all dollkind."

Nobody disagreed with her.

The dolls sat silently in the hut until, from somewhere in BJ's house, they heard a clock chime.

"Four-thirty," said Beth, sounding concerned. "We can't wait any longer. We have to start cleaning up. This is probably going to take all night."

"We'll look for Carl while we work," said Waterfall.

"Has he ever escaped before?" asked Tiffany.

"Nope. This is the first time."

"Have you ever even touched Carl?" asked Annabelle.

138

"No. And I'd rather not think about that. We don't have a choice. We *have* to try to put Carl back in his cage if we find him. So let's get started."

"How can you stand this?" asked Tiffany. "Mean Mimi causes trouble for you every weekend, and then *you* have to clean up *her* messes."

"Like I said," Waterfall replied, "we don't have a choice."

Annabelle, Tiffany, the Cutouts, the PJ Party Pals, and the Troll Twins left the safety of the hut and peered cautiously around BJ's room. There was no sign of Carl.

"All right. Let's get started," said Yvonne.

"We don't know where things go," Tiffany pointed out, "so you'll have to tell Annabelle and me what to do."

The dolls worked side by side for hours. No one spoke except to say "The cars all have to go back to Callie's room" or "Help me take this barricade apart" or "Just leave those things there. I think they were already on the floor." And every now and then someone would scream, "There he is! There's Carl!" and then realize it was one of BJ's plastic lizards.

It was early Sunday morning, the sun streaming through BJ's windows and brightening his room, when Tiffany caught sight of Carl.

"There he is! There's Carl!" she cried. "This time I really do see him!"

Tiffany pointed to the windowsill above Carl's cage, and sure enough, the lizard was basking in the warm sunlight.

Annabelle was both terrified and relieved to see him. She didn't know where he had been all night, but it didn't really matter. "All right, everybody," she said. "We have to get him back in his cage. How are we going to do it?"

Nobody wanted to touch Carl. And nobody wanted to hurt him.

"Do you think," said Annabelle after a moment, "that if the Cutouts tickled Carl, it might scare him and he would fall down into his cage?"

"It's worth a try," said Penny.

"Oh, yes, it's worth a try," sang the

Cutouts. And they began to make their way up the curtain that hung at the window.

Annabelle noticed that they wisely climbed up the left-hand side, which was near the tip of Carl's tail—as far as possible from his eyes. She watched those eyes very closely, and decided that maybe Carl was napping. She hoped so, because without warning, the Cutout at the bottom of the chain suddenly let go of the curtain and swung away from it, sweeping along Carl's tail with her free hand.

Carl wriggled. Then, startled, he jumped.

"Pull me back!" squealed the Cutout, but it wasn't necessary. In his confusion, Carl lost his balance and tumbled off the windowsill and into his cage below.

"Good work!" cried Melody.

All the dolls rushed to the cage to look in at Carl. He seemed to be unhurt, and resumed his nap.

"All right, now we have to put the top back on the tank," said Yvonne.

The other dolls groaned. The tank was much taller than any of them, and the lid was too heavy for them to lift easily.

"You know what?" said Waterfall. "I don't think I can do a single other thing. This is just too much."

Melody glared at her, then said, "Okay, but this has to get done. If you don't want to help us, go sit in the hut. Anyone want to join her?" she asked the others.

The dolls shook their heads. And Annabelle cringed, but she understood why Melody had spoken sharply. "This is getting desperate," she whispered to Tiffany. "What time is it?"

"I don't know. Midmorning, I guess. Look at this room."

Annabelle nodded. It was still a mess. Carl had been caught, thank goodness, but hoisting the top back onto the tank was probably going to take hours. And the race-track still had to be taken apart and put away.

Waterfall was slinking off to the Lego hut

when Annabelle heard a noise behind her and turned to see the Sandra doll lope into the room, holding her blanket in one hand and leading Sleeping Billy along with the other. She stood in the mess, looking hopefully at the smaller dolls.

"Sandra?" said Melody.

The Sandra doll offered a smile.

"Did Mimi send you in here?"

She shook her head.

"Can we help you with something?"

The Sandra doll gazed around at the messy room. Then she looked back at Melody.

"I'm not sure I understand," said Melody.

"I think I do," Annabelle said. "Sandra wants to help us clean up. Don't you, Sandra?"

The Sandra doll smiled again. Then she let go of Sleeping Billy's hand and picked up a book that had been knocked from the shelf. She set it in place.

"Ooh," said the PJ Party Pals.

Melody brightened. "Could you put the top back on Carl's tank?" she asked.

The Sandra doll crossed the room to the tank and replaced the top.

"Thanks, thanks, our undying thanks," sang the Cutouts.

"Yes, thank you," said the other dolls.

Tiffany looked at Sleeping Billy. "What about him?" she asked the Sandra doll. "Will he help too?"

When the Sandra doll had let go of his hand, Sleeping Billy had slid onto his side and fallen asleep. Now she straightened him up and showed him how to take the racetrack apart.

"This is great!" exclaimed Beth. "We'll have everything cleaned up in no time."

Melody called Waterfall out of the Lego hut and apologized to her. Then the dolls set to work, and just as Beth had predicted, the room was cleaned up quickly.

"I think this is the best it's ever looked on a Sunday," said Yvonne. "It's almost exactly as BJ left it."

Except for the rip and the nick and a few other things, thought Annabelle. But she said nothing.

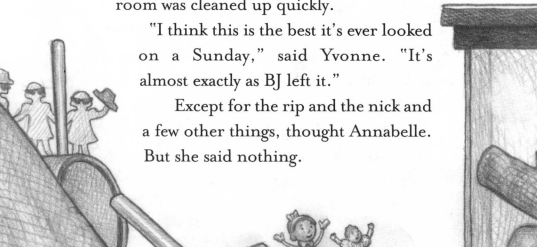

"Where are all of you supposed to be?" Tiffany asked the dolls. "In Callie's room?"

"Yes," replied Penny. "We'll go over there this afternoon."

"And we'll climb into BJ's backpack," said Annabelle. "Does he take it to school every day?"

"Just about," said Beth.

"Good," Annabelle replied. "Then we'll be back in our house tomorrow. Home sweet home."

"Home sweet home," a mocking voice repeated from the doorway.

Annabelle jumped when she

heard Mean Mimi, and stumbled backward. Tiffany caught her, steadied her, and marched boldly across the room until she was standing just inches away from Mimi.

"No one's afraid of you anymore, you know," said Tiffany.

"She is," Mean Mimi replied, pointing at Annabelle.

"But she'll be gone tomorrow. You have no power here."

"I do too!" cried Mimi. "I—I have, um—"

"You have nothing," said Tiffany. "Everyone knows about Techno-Man now. And the Sandra doll and Sleeping Billy would rather be friends than fight."

"You—you can't do this to the Queen of All Dolls!"

"But we did do it."

For a few seconds, Tiffany and Mean Mimi stood facing one another. Mimi glared her fiercest glare, but Tiffany never looked away from her. At last Mimi turned and stomped down the hall.

Then Waterfall said what the other dolls were truly thinking. "She may not have any control over us, but we don't have any control over her, either. She's reckless. She'll do anything, anything, to get what she wants. She is still a menace to all dollkind."

"To all dollkind, all dollkind," whispered the Cutouts as they slipped out of BJ's room and disappeared into the hall. "A menace to all dollkind."

CHAPTER ELEVEN

The Return

FOR SEVERAL more hours Annabelle, Tiffany, and Callie's dolls sat quietly in BJ's bedroom. They saw no sign of Mean Mimi and no sign of Techno-Man.

"Pretty soon we'll have to go back to Callie's room," said Melody, standing and stretching. "Mimi is going to be madder than a hornet, but once Callie comes home she won't be able to do anything to us."

"So she behaves herself when Callie's around?" asked Annabelle.

"Well, mostly," said Melody, and

Annabelle felt fear ripple through her. How much damage could Mimi cause?

"What about Techno-Man?" asked Tiffany. "Where do you think he is?"

"I'm not sure," replied Melody. "This makes me nervous. Techno-Man was humiliated. He was embarrassed. So I guess he's off sulking. He's never done that before. I hope he has the sense to return before BJ and Callie do."

"Whose room does he belong in?" Annabelle wanted to know.

"BJ's. See that bucket in the corner? That's where the action figures are kept. Although . . . I wonder if Techno-Man will stay there now, since we know he isn't an action figure, after all."

The dolls sat and talked until finally Waterfall said, "I think we should go." She looked at Annabelle and Tiffany. "We hate to leave you, but we want to be ready when Callie comes home."

"That's okay. We should get in the backpack anyway," replied Tiffany.

Beth let out a loud sigh. "Back to Mimi Land."

The dolls stood up. They hugged each other and called good-bye.

"When we get home," Annabelle said, "we're going to tell our parents about Mean Mimi. She really is a menace. Maybe they'll have some ideas about what to do."

"It must be nice to have grown-up dolls around," said Penny.

"It is," Annabelle replied. "Mostly."

The Troll Twins, the PJ Party Pals, the Cutouts, the Sandra doll, and Sleeping Billy left the room.

"Okay," said Tiffany. "Into the backpack?"

"Into the backpack," said Annabelle.

She and Tiffany waded through the toys

and papers on the floor, which Annabelle prayed were now in exactly the same spots in which they had been when BJ left on Friday. Then they stood before the backpack and looked at it. Like Kate's, there was one large main compartment, and several smaller zippered ones on the outside.

"Where should we hide?" asked Tiffany.

"The big compartment," said Annabelle promptly. "We'll stay at the bottom like we did when we were in Kate's."

And so Annabelle and Tiffany spent a long night at the bottom of BJ's backpack. They crawled under some papers and an old woolen glove, and then they listened. They listened to the sounds of BJ's family returning home late that afternoon. They listened to voices calling, and thought they knew now whose was BJ's and whose was Callie's and whose were their parents'. They listened especially hard for any signs that the humans thought things were not quite right, but they heard nothing disturbing.

Later, much later, they listened to nighttime sounds, and heard many that were familiar to them—the hum of the refrigerator, clocks ticking, floors creaking. They heard a scrabbling sound too, and thought maybe BJ's house had mice, which upset Annabelle, but the scrabbling stopped and no mice jumped into the backpack, so Annabelle stopped worrying and thought instead about the wonderful homecoming they would soon have.

By the morning a new set of worries occupied Annabelle. What if BJ didn't take his backpack to school? Would she and Tiffany have time to climb out of the pack and find something else in which to hide? What if BJ did take his backpack but he went searching for his glove and found Annabelle and Tiffany instead? What if the girls got to school safely but *Kate* hadn't brought *her* backpack that day? What if they made it all the way back to the Palmers' house only to discover that their absence had been noted, and that Kate and Nora had been searching for them and now the humans were suspicious?

But Annabelle's worries were for nothing. BJ did pick up the backpack and take it to school. During a quiet moment that morning, the girls managed to slip out of it, drop to the floor, find Kate's pack (this time they made *certain* it was hers), and climb into it. At the end of the day, the bell rang, and presently Annabelle heard Kate's voice as she hoisted the backpack from its shelf and slid her arms through the straps. Twenty minutes later Annabelle and Tiffany were back in the Palmers' house on Wetherby Lane. Kate set the backpack on the kitchen floor while she ate a snack with Nora and Grandma Katherine.

Then she carried the pack upstairs to her room and dropped it on her bed. A few minutes later Annabelle heard footsteps leave the room, then Kate calling, "Grandma Katherine? Can I go over to Ayanna's house?"

When the dolls heard only silence for the next few minutes, they could wait no longer.

"Now?" Annabelle whispered to Tiffany.

"Now." Annabelle could tell that Tiffany was grinning.

"You should probably come to my house," said Annabelle as she stood up. "You shouldn't risk being seen in the Palmers' hallway. It's dangerous enough to run across Kate's room at this time of day."

"That's okay. I'll go back to my house tonight."

The dolls scrambled out of the pack and crawled down Kate's bedspread to the floor. Then they dashed across the room to the step stool. They stood at the bottom of it and called softly, "Hello? Anybody home?"

For a moment they heard nothing. Then a voice replied, "Annabelle? Tiffany? Is that you?"

"Yes, it's us! It's really us!" Annabelle cried softly.

Cautiously, Mama and Papa appeared at the front of the dollhouse. Mama glanced around Kate's room, checking to make sure no humans were in sight.

To Annabelle's surprise, Mom Funcraft appeared next to Papa. So Nora's been playing in Kate's room again, thought Annabelle. That was probably a good thing.

"Oh! Oh, dear," said Mama, looking faint. "We were afraid we might never see you again. Are you all right? Are you really all right?"

"Yes, we're fine," replied Annabelle.

"Hi, honey!" Mom Funcraft called to Tiffany. "Did you have fun?"

"Well, my land!" exclaimed Nanny, peering over Mama's shoulder.

"What— Where—" Uncle Doll spluttered.

And Auntie Sarah said, "*There* you are,

girls. Good heavens, come on up here."

Annabelle and Tiffany scrambled up the steps to the dollhouse as fast as they were able. A few moments later Annabelle felt herself caught up in a flurry of hugs, wrapped in first her mother's arms, then her father's,

then Auntie Sarah's, then Uncle Doll's, then Nanny's, then Mom Funcraft's, then Bobby's, and finally even Baby Betsy's, as she reached out from her spot on the floor.

"Where on *earth* have you been?" asked
Mama, motioning the dolls to move to the
back of the house.

"Why, they've been to school, I pre-
sume," said Auntie Sarah. "Isn't that right,
girls?"

"Yes, and—" Annabelle started to reply.

"My, what an adventure!" said Mom
Funcraft.

"But why didn't you come back on

Thursday?" asked Papa. "Kate brought her pack home with her. We saw her." Annabelle heard a hint of annoyance in his voice.

Tiffany must have heard it too, because she said, "We tried to come home then, we really did. But we had gotten out of Kate's pack in school and then we couldn't return to it in time—"

"You got out of the pack?" repeated Mama in alarm. "Why?"

And Uncle Doll said, "You ran around a big place like *school*? In front of all those *humans*?"

Annabelle elbowed Tiffany, realizing they should have spent some of the hours stuck in BJ's backpack discussing what they were going to tell their parents.

Tiffany abruptly stopped speaking.

But Auntie Sarah said, "Ah, school. Just think . . . To be in an actual *school* . . . My, my."

"Sarah!" said Uncle Doll sharply. "Don't encourage them."

"Oh, for heaven's sake. I'm sure

they were careful. What a wonderful opportunity for an Exploration. An Exploration of some magnitude, I might add."

"I'll say," agreed Mom Funcraft.

"We were careful," said Annabelle meekly.

"Very careful," added Tiffany.

Auntie Sarah was rubbing her hands together with relish. "All right. So you were stuck in school on Thursday night. Then what happened? What happened on Friday?"

"You really are not going to believe it," said Tiffany.

"What? What?" cried Auntie Sarah and Mom Funcraft at the same time.

Annabelle had been trying to figure out just what to say and what not to say in order to stay out of trouble. But now she had a feeling that, with Auntie Sarah and Mom Funcraft on their side, she and Tiffany weren't going to be in much trouble, anyway.

"Okay. On Friday," said Tiffany, "we waited for just the right moment to return to Kate's backpack."

Together, Tiffany and Annabelle began the story of their adventure. They told of accidentally climbing in BJ's backpack, of peering out of the pack later and realizing they were in the wrong house, of meeting their new friends, of Mean Mimi, and of the terrible trouble they thought dollkind might now be in. They told the story in turns. Tiffany would speak until she left something out, then Annabelle would jump in. Annabelle would speak until she left something out, then Tiffany would jump in.

When they finished their story, the other dolls were speechless. They looked both astonished and frightened. Mama and Papa clutched each other, and Uncle Doll fanned himself with his handkerchief. "All my life I've been afraid of something like this," he said, with a small moan.

"Imagine, such a menace so nearby," whispered Nanny.

"Mama," said Annabelle, "Papa, do you think there's any way we can help Melody and Waterfall and the other dolls at BJ's? They're in trouble—"

"Huge trouble," added Tiffany.

"And so are we. So are dolls everywhere," said Annabelle.

The grown-ups looked at one another.

"Annabelle—" Mama said, but she was interrupted by a noise from across the room.

All the dolls jumped.

"Places! Places, everyone!" hissed Papa. "Annabelle and Tiffany, hide!"

"Oh, there's no need for that," a voice called. "It's just me."

As Annabelle and the others watched, one of the small compartments on Kate's backpack opened and a doll dressed in

lavender climbed out, scurried down the bed, and began to cross the floor toward the doll-house.

It was Mean Mimi.

CHAPTER TWELVE

Who's Sorry Now?

AUGHHHHHH!!"shrieked Annabelle.

And Tiffany cried, "It's Mean Mimi!" just as Annabelle exclaimed, "It's Princess Mimi!"

The sparkly figure trotted across the rug. The sight of Mimi flitting through Kate Palmer's bedroom in her lavender clothes made Annabelle's knees buckle, and she had to sit down. The last time she had seen her, Mimi had been angry—angry because she realized she could no longer control the dolls at BJ's house. And Annabelle had felt a teeny bit better, knowing that Melody and the others would no longer be bullied. But what was it Waterfall had said? That the other dolls had no control over Mimi? Yes. And that because she was reckless, she was still a menace to all dollkind.

And now here was the menace, in Annabelle's very home.

Annabelle gripped Tiffany's arm and waited for Mimi to break something or tear something, to do anything that would later attract Kate's attention. But Mimi only hurried to the bottom of the stool, then climbed the steps as if she had been doing it for years. By the time she had reached the Dolls' house, however, Annabelle saw that tears were brimming in her eyes.

"Are—are you the Dolls?" asked Mimi timidly.

Annabelle, her family, Tiffany, and Mom Funcraft had gathered uncertainly at the front of the house, Uncle Doll and Nanny hovering behind the others.

"Yes," said Papa. "And are you Mea— Are you Princess Mimi?"

"I am," she replied formally. "Princess Mimi . . . the small and meek."

Annabelle frowned. The small and meek? Where had she heard that before? Oh, yes. In *The Wizard of Oz,* a movie Annabelle had seen in its entirety one night when Kate was having a sleepover downstairs in the living room. Dorothy, trying to convince the Wizard that she was not a threat, had introduced herself to him as "Dorothy, the small and meek."

Annabelle glanced at Tiffany. "The small and meek?" she whispered disdainfully, and Tiffany made a face.

"What are you doing here?" Auntie Sarah asked Mimi suspiciously. "And how did you get here? Did you follow Annabelle and Tiffany?"

Mimi nodded, and Annabelle noticed that she appeared just barely able to keep her tears from overflowing and running down her plastic cheeks.

"Yes," said Mimi. "I climbed into BJ's backpack after they did. I hid in a different compartment. And today in school, I followed them to the other backpack. Maybe I shouldn't have, but—"

"I'll say she shouldn't have," Tiffany whispered.

"—but I need a new home, and Tiffany and Annabelle talked about theirs, and it sounded so wonderful . . . with grown-ups and all . . ."

"Why do you need a new home?" asked Mom Funcraft.

"Because—because nobody likes me at Callie's house. The other dolls are all mean to me. They tease me and gang up on me and—and I didn't do anything!" she wailed. "Not anything at all."

"Then why are they mean to you?" asked Bobby.

Good question, thought Annabelle.

"I don't know!" Mimi began to sob.

166

"They just are. Maybe because they're jealous. Jealous that I'm a princess, and I have such beautiful clothes. Or maybe because I don't have a mom or a dad. I'm—I'm an orphan."

"The PJ Party Pals and the Troll Twins and the Cutouts don't have parents either," pointed out Tiffany.

"But they have each other," said Mean Mimi, sniffing loudly. "I have no one."

"Poor little girl," Mama murmured. "No home, no family."

"Yes, poor little girl," said Papa.

Auntie Sarah pursed her lips together, though, and glanced sharply from Mimi to Annabelle and Tiffany.

"You must stay with us for the time being," Mama said kindly to Mimi.

"What?!" cried Annabelle.

"What?!" cried Tiffany.

"Girls, manners," said Nanny softly.

"But—but," spluttered Tiffany, "didn't you hear what we said before? Mimi was putting Callie's dolls in jeopardy. She was putting *all* dolls in jeopardy—doing things that couldn't be fixed."

Mimi covered her eyes with her hands and sobbed more loudly than ever. "See? This is just what I was talking about! Nobody likes me. Everybody hates me. They say I'm a horrible person, but I'm not! I'm not!"

Mean Mimi crumpled into a little heap by the top step of the stool.

Annabelle looked down in horror as her own mother knelt beside Mimi and put her arms around her.

But Auntie Sarah said, "Mimi *will* have to stay with us, that's true. We must hide her. We can't let Kate discover a strange doll here. That's far too risky."

"A home at last," said Mimi from the floor.

"A hiding place," said Auntie Sarah firmly. "That is all."

"For heaven's sake," muttered Papa.

"We'll discuss this later," said Auntie Sarah. "Tonight. When the Palmers are asleep. We'll have to come up with a permanent solution."

"Oh, anything, anything!" exclaimed Mimi. "Just don't make me go back to Callie's room."

"We'll see," said Auntie Sarah. "For now . . . hmm, I wonder where we could hide you."

Mean Mimi was bigger than Annabelle and Tiffany, but she wasn't any bigger than Baby Betsy. Annabelle tried to think of the places in her house in which Baby Betsy could fit. There weren't many. But Nora had once managed to stuff Baby Betsy underneath Mama and Papa's high bed.

"Let's stick her under your bed," said Annabelle to her parents.

Mean Mimi wrinkled her nose.

"Isn't there anyplace else?" asked Mama, looking sympathetically at Mimi.

"Why can't I just sit somewhere?" asked Mimi.

"In *plain view*?" said Auntie Sarah. "Because Kate will see you, that's why. And she'll want to know where you came from. She'll be suspicious."

"I suppose she could hide somewhere in Kate's room," said Nanny.

"We'll have to choose a place where Kate doesn't go very often," said Papa.

"Very often?" repeated Mimi. "How long am I going to hide?"

"For heaven's sake, let's stop talking about this and just do something," said Mom Funcraft. "Mimi dear, why don't you go sit in the Barbie camper? You'll be safe there."

"Hmphh," said Uncle Doll, who had once run away to the camper and didn't like to be reminded of it.

Mimi's eyes filled with tears once more.

"I—I— Why are you kicking me out? I don't understand. Don't you want me—"

From the hallway came the sound of voices. "Mom?"

"That's Kate!" Annabelle whispered loudly. "She's back from Ayanna's house! The Palmers must be home, too."

"Hi, honey," said Mrs. Palmer. "Dinner in half an hour. How much homework do you have tonight?"

"I have to study my spelling words," Kate replied.

"Why don't you do that now? I'll call you when dinner's ready."

Papa Doll looked as though he were about to faint. "Places, everyone! Places right now!"

"But Mimi isn't—" Annabelle cried.

"No time, no time," said Uncle Doll with a gasp.

In a flash, Mama sat down on a kitchen chair; Papa, Bobby, and Mom

Funcraft threw themselves to the parlor floor; Uncle Doll and Auntie Sarah arranged themselves in their bedroom; and Nanny stood stiffly beside Baby Betsy, who was still seated where Kate had last left her.

Annabelle and Tiffany, who didn't know where they were supposed to be, joined the heap of dolls in the parlor.

"Hide! Hide!" Tiffany said desperately to Mean Mimi. "Anywhere! Just hide. Now."

Annabelle, at the top of the heap of dolls, rolled over a teeny bit so that she could look into Kate's room. She glanced from Mean Mimi, still standing on the top step of the stool, to the doorway, waiting to see Kate.

"GO!" cried Tiffany.

And Mimi disappeared from view as she scrambled back down the stool. Annabelle could see the top of the Barbie camper, and she expected the door to open, then shut, as Mimi rushed inside.

But the door remained closed.

Annabelle heard footsteps in the hall, heard Kate say, "Not now, Nora. I have to look at my spelling words. We're going to have a quiz tomorrow."

"She's right down the hall!" exclaimed Annabelle.

And that was when she saw Mean Mimi run lightly across Kate's room and out into the Palmers' house.

CHAPTER THIRTEEN

The Queen of Mean

ANNABELLE waited for a shriek, for a scream, for Kate or Nora to wail, "I saw a doll! I saw a doll running in the hall!" She waited for the grown-ups to be called. She waited to see if she would go into Doll State for this.

But the hallway was quiet. A moment later, Kate walked through her doorway, flopped onto her bed, rummaged around in her backpack, pulled out her spelling book, and began reciting, "Question—Q-U-E-S-T-I-O-N. Experiment—E-X-P-E-R-I-M-E-N-T. Possible—P-O-S-S-I-B-L-E."

Annabelle should have felt relieved, but she didn't. Where was Mimi? Annabelle didn't know how Mimi had managed to escape being seen by Kate or any of the Palmers, but apparently she had, and she wasn't in Kate's room, which meant she was just loose in the house.

For the next six hours Annabelle worried in silence. Worried and waited. Waited for her father to get to his feet and give the all-clear signal. When he finally did, the Dolls and Mom Funcraft gathered in the parlor and talked in hushed, excited voices.

"Where do you think she is?"

"She could be anywhere."

"She doesn't know the humans who live here. She doesn't know their routines."

"I can't believe she would do such a thing."

Nobody had to say who "she" was.

"Annabelle, Tiffany," said Mama, "tell

us again what happened when you were at BJ's house this weekend. *Exactly* what happened."

The girls told the story a second time, trying to be as specific about Mean Mimi as possible. They told how Mimi had controlled the Sandra doll and Sleeping Billy and Techno-Man. They told how the Sandra doll and Sleeping Billy and Techno-Man were no longer on Mimi's side, which meant that Mimi no longer had any friends. ("If you can call people who are afraid of you your friends," said Tiffany.) They told about the havoc Mimi could wreak when the humans were away, and how some of it couldn't be fixed. They mentioned that BJ's family was starting to become suspicious.

"Which means that other humans are probably already suspicious," said Uncle Doll. "And suspicion spreads quickly."

"Suspicions are insidious," said Papa, and Annabelle rolled the word *insidious* around in her head, thinking that she must remember to ask someone about it later.

Once again the conclusion was reached that dollkind was in jeopardy.

"And now the cause of all this trouble is here in the Palmers' house," said Mama.

Auntie Sarah looked thoughtful. "But I believe," she said after a moment, "that we are stronger than she is."

"Right is might," said Mom Funcraft.

"Usually," said Nanny.

"The question is," said Papa, "what are we going to *do* about Mimi?"

"We have to find her and get her back home," said Annabelle.

"How on earth are we going to do that?" asked Mama.

"Yeah, even if we catch her, how will we get her back to BJ's?" asked Tiffany.

"I'm not sure she should go back to BJ's," said Uncle Doll. "She's too much of a menace."

"Well, she has to be somewhere," said Nanny. "And I don't think we want her here."

"Plus, if she doesn't go back to BJ's, Callie is going to wonder what happened to her," pointed out Annabelle. "Mimi is Callie's favorite doll. Waterfall said Callie plays with her nearly every day. Mimi is putting dolls in jeopardy just by disappearing from her home."

"Then I think we have to decide what is worse," said Mom Funcraft. "How will Mimi do the most damage? By running around in a strange house where she might be noticed by the humans, or by disappearing from Callie's?"

"Before we decide what to do with her, we'd better catch her," said Bobby sensibly.

Annabelle leaned toward Tiffany and whispered, "Is this a job for SELMP?"

"I think it's too big for SELMP." Tiffany looked nervous, which made Annabelle *very* nervous. What had happened to her fearless friend?

"Maybe I should get my husband," said Mom Funcraft. "He'll want to be involved in our discussion. I'm not positive where Nora has left him, but he's probably at home with Bailey and Baby Britney."

It was decided that Annabelle and Tiffany would accompany Mom Funcraft down the hall to Nora's room. The three dolls tiptoed across Kate's floor and paused in her doorway.

Annabelle hadn't felt so nervous in the Palmers' house since the days when The Captain used to roam freely. Holding tightly to Tiffany with her left hand and to Mom Funcraft with her right, she peered around the corner and looked both ways in the hall. "I don't see anything," she whispered.

"Me neither," said Tiffany.

"Okay, let's go." Mom Funcraft led the way.

Hugging the wall, they crept in single file through the darkness toward Nora's room.

Would it be like this from now on? wondered Annabelle. Had the dolls lost their freedom? They had grown used to being able to run through the upstairs of the Palmers' house, The Captain safely banished to the first floor. As long as they kept an eye out for the humans, and as long as they returned to wherever they were supposed to be when the humans were awake, Annabelle and Tiffany had felt free to spend hours visiting with one another, going on Explorations with Auntie Sarah, playing games with their brothers. Now, Annabelle realized, that might come to an end. She found herself waiting for Mean Mimi to loom out of the darkness, to fire a missile at them. She feared Mimi might discover and awaken some sleepy, dusty, forgotten doll and enlist it in a fight against the Dolls and the Funcrafts.

A cat toy was the last thing Annabelle expected. When one rolled down the hall toward them, its bell tinkling impossibly loudly, Annabelle felt as if she were a pin about to be bowled over.

"Yikes!" Tiffany let out the quietest shriek she could manage.

"What's that?" cried Mom Funcraft.

"One of The Captain's toys," said Annabelle, jumping aside as the plastic ball bumped to a stop against the wall.

"Where did it come from?"

"Hee, hee."

Annabelle heard laughter from the other end of the hall. "It's Mimi! It's Mimi!" she yelped.

"Shhhh!" said Mom Funcraft, and she pulled Annabelle and Tiffany through Nora's doorway, across the floor of her room, and into the pink dollhouse.

"Hello?" called Dad Funcraft from upstairs. "Hello?"

"Dad, it's us!" Tiffany called back, but a ringing bell drowned out her voice. The Captain's toy hurtled through Nora's room and lodged under her bed.

"She's going to wake up! She's going to wake up!" hissed Annabelle, peering at the dark shape on Nora's bed. But nothing moved.

Dad Funcraft ran down the stairs of the pink dollhouse. "Girls! You're home!" He

hugged Tiffany, then Annabelle. "Where were you? We were so worried! When did you get back? What happened? Did you have adven—"

"Dear," Mom Funcraft interrupted him, "we have a small problem." She tried to explain to him—quickly and very quietly—who Mean Mimi was and what was happening. "Come to the Dolls' house with us," she said.

"We need to have a neighborhood meeting right away."

"Hee, hee."

Mean Mimi's laughter floated to their ears from Nora's doorway, but no matter how hard Annabelle stared through the darkness, she couldn't see her.

"All right," said Dad Funcraft, glancing toward the door. "A meeting sounds like a good idea. But I think we should leave Baby Britney here. I'd rather not carry her through the hall if that doll is loose."

"She's right outside the door," Annabelle hissed. "I'm positive."

"Then, Annabelle, you and Tiffany stay here with Bailey and Baby Britney. You can hide in the house."

"No!" shrieked Annabelle.

And Tiffany said, "We're not going to stay here by ourselves! She'll find us!"

Mom and Dad Funcraft looked at each other.

"All right. Everybody come with us," said Mom. "Maybe we'll be safer as a group."

Huddled together, Dad Funcraft carrying Baby Britney, the dolls ventured through

Nora's room. Annabelle put her hands over her eyes as she turned the corner into the hallway. She waited to be hit with something, to be bowled over by something, to hear the chilling "Hee, hee." But the hall now seemed empty. The dolls dashed along it and into Kate's room.

"We made it!" Tiffany exclaimed softly, just as the cat toy was fired through the doorway

behind them. It crashed to a stop against the leg of Kate's desk.

Annabelle heard muffled cries from her house.

"Hurry! Hurry!" called Mom Funcraft.

Annabelle and Tiffany each grabbed one of Bailey's hands, and they ran toward the step stool on the heels of Mom, Dad, and Baby Britney.

"Yo! Loyal subjects! Hee, hee!"

Annabelle spun around and now she could see Mean Mimi clearly. She stood in a patch of moonlight, grinning at the dolls, her lavender clothes glittering.

"We are not your loyal subjects," said Tiffany, letting go of Bailey's hand and facing Mimi.

Mom Funcraft stood beside Tiffany. "And please be quiet," she said in a low voice. "You'll wake Kate and then you'll end up in Doll State."

"We might all end up in Doll State," called Auntie Sarah from above.

"Doll State, ha!" said Mean Mimi. "There's no such thing."

Annabelle started to say, There is, too. I've been in it.

But Mimi continued, "Anyway, I think it's time for me to let Kate in on a little secret." She ran to the head of Kate's bed and looked up. "Kate! Wake up, Kate!" she called—in a voice so loud Annabelle and Tiffany would have used it only if the Palmers'

house had been completely empty. "Your dollies are alive. They're alive!"

In her bed, Kate stirred, then rolled over. Annabelle held her breath, willing Kate to stay asleep, and she did.

"Hmphh," said Mimi and ran from the room.

The moment she was out of sight, Annabelle, Tiffany, Bailey, and Mom and Dad Funcraft with Baby Britney made their way up the steps of the stool and huddled in the Dolls' parlor.

Kate slept soundly.

After a long, long silence Uncle Doll, his head in his hands, said, "What are we going to do?"

No one answered.

Annabelle pulled Tiffany aside and whispered, "You know what Mean Mimi is doing, don't you? She's getting revenge on us. We took away her friends, we changed her life at BJ's, so now she's going to ruin things here. She plans to reveal our secret lives to Kate."

CHAPTER FOURTEEN

A Neighborhood Meeting

THE DOLLS AND the Funcrafts
had held two previous neighborhood
meetings. The first had taken place
several months earlier after Tiffany
had overheard a discussion in
which she thought the Palmers had
decided to get a dog. The second
one had taken place the previous
day, and Annabelle and Tiffany
had known nothing about it.
Their families had met to discuss
what they should do if the girls
didn't return very soon. Now the

girls were back, and the families needed to meet again.

"To get rid of the menace we brought with us," said Annabelle, feeling guilty.

The meeting was held in the Dolls' parlor, the seven grown-ups crowded onto chairs and the sofa. Annabelle, Tiffany, Bobby, and Bailey sat on the floor. (Baby Betsy and Baby Britney had been settled with quiet toys in the

dining room where Nanny could keep her eye on them.) At first everyone tried to face out into Kate's room so they could watch for Mean Mimi, but it was very difficult to carry on a conversation when everyone was looking in the same direction. Eventually, Annabelle, Tiffany, Bailey, and Bobby turned around and faced the grown-ups, but Annabelle found herself constantly glancing over her shoulder.

Auntie Sarah led the meeting.

"I hereby call to order this the third meeting of the Neighborhood Doll Association," she said. "Tonight we have gathered to discuss the problem of Mimi. Is it agreed that our first order of business is to figure out a way in which to capture Mimi? If so, say Aye."

"Aye," the dolls called softly.

"Very good," said Auntie Sarah. "Okay, any ideas?"

Tiffany shot her hand in the air. "Ooh! Ooh! I have an idea."

"Tiffany?" Auntie Sarah pointed to her.

"I think," said Tiffany, "that we should trick Mean Mimi into meeting up with The Captain."

The dolls glanced at one another.

"Okay . . ." said Auntie Sarah.

"I don't get it," said Bailey.

"Well, see, we'll use reverse psychology," Tiffany explained. "We'll wait until we see Mimi again. Then we'll tell her that we don't care what she does in this house as long as she doesn't hurt the poor kitty downstairs. Like in the story about Br'er Rabbit and the briar patch. Then Mimi will go downstairs just to do what we told her *not* to do—and The Captain will get her." Tiffany sat back, looking pleased.

"What do you mean, he'll get her?" asked Annabelle.

"He'll run off with her, like he did with . . . with you, Mr. Doll."

"But I thought *we* were supposed to capture Mimi," said Bobby.

Everyone looked at Auntie Sarah. "Well," she said, "I guess that's what I meant. Although I'm not sure what we'll do with Mimi once we catch her."

"Still, we don't want The Captain to catch her, do we?" asked Annabelle. "For one thing, Mimi might hurt him. I know we don't like The Captain, but we don't want him to get hurt. And what would the humans think had happened to him? Plus, Mimi would probably just escape from him, and then we'd be right back where we started." Annabelle paused. "I'm sorry, Tiffany. I think that's a clever idea. I really do. But I'm not sure it would work out in the end."

After a moment Papa Doll said, "I think it's clear that we have to set this trap ourselves. I'm just not sure what kind of trap it should be."

"Maybe something involving a spider's web," said Auntie Sarah thoughtfully. "Spiders' webs are very strong, you know. Strong enough to ensnare large wriggling insects."

"But strong enough to ensnare a large wriggling doll?" asked Annabelle.

"Well, maybe strong enough to ensnare her while we tie her up with rope. We could do it in the attic where no one would come upon her."

"And then we would bring her downstairs all tied up?" asked Nanny.

"Well, I don't know. . . ."

The members of the NDA sat thoughtfully, the grown-ups staring out into Kate's
room. Finally, Auntie Sarah said, "Perhaps
we should move on to the second order of
business—what should we do with Mimi if we
catch her?"

The grown-ups twisted their hands.
Tiffany played with the bow in her hair. Bailey
and Bobby tapped their feet. Annabelle
looked thoughtful.

"We could turn the Barbie
camper into a jail," said Papa Doll
after a few moments. "We could
leave her tied up in there until we
think she's learned her lesson."

"I suppose that could work,"
said Uncle Doll. "As long as Kate
doesn't happen to look in the
camper. I'm not sure we can count on
Mimi to keep quiet, though."

"What if," said Mama, "we treated Mimi
with kindness while she was in the camper?
Perhaps people haven't been very kind to
her."

"Can you blame them?" whispered
Tiffany to Annabelle.

"That's an interesting idea," said Mom Funcraft. "Maybe she would learn to change her ways."

"I like the idea of trapping her in the camper," said Nanny, "but I don't think she needs kindness, I think she needs discipline."

"Discipline can be administered with kindness," said Auntie Sarah.

"Hmphh," said Nanny.

Bailey raised his hand.

"Bailey?" said Auntie Sarah.

"I bet Mean Mimi doesn't know how to have fun," he said. "Maybe she needs fun. Like in that song—girls just wanna have fun."

"Yes! More quality fun," said Dad Funcraft.

"Plus, trapping her would be fun for us," added Bobby.

"That doll does not need fun, she needs REFORM!" thundered Uncle Doll, and everyone quickly turned their attention to Kate, but she slept on. Uncle Doll composed himself. "Pardon me," he said.

"So what exactly are we going to do?" asked Mom Funcraft.

"Let's take turns voicing our opinions individually," replied Auntie Sarah. "I'd like to hear from each one of you. Quietly," she added, looking at Uncle Doll.

"Okay, I'll start," said Dad Funcraft. "I think we should trap Mimi, but I'm not sure how—I don't know that the spider's web idea is going to work. Then after we trap her, we bring her to the Barbie camper and teach her how to have fun. She needs to let her hair down a little."

"I agree with Dad," said Mom Funcraft.

"I think," said Mama Doll, "that we should trap her somehow—I'm not sure about the spider's web either—and take her to the camper where we'll show her kindness."

"I agree with Mama," said Papa Doll.

"I think we should take her to the camper for discipline," said Nanny.

"I agree with Nanny," said Uncle Doll.

"I don't really care what we do with her as long as we trap her," said Bobby.

"Yeah," agreed Bailey and Tiffany.

"Hmm. Clearly, we'll have to give more thought to setting a trap," said Auntie Sarah.

"Annabelle? What do you think we should do?"

Everyone turned to Annabelle.

"I think . . ." said Annabelle softly. She hesitated. "I think that before we do anything we should all take deep breaths."

"What?" said several of the dolls after a moment of uncomfortable silence.

"We need to take deep breaths," Annabelle repeated patiently. "What Mimi is doing to us is terrible. She's trying to make us afraid—afraid to move about, afraid to live our lives, afraid to be free. But we don't have to let her. No one can *make* us feel anything. We are the only ones who control what we feel. So we can choose not to feel afraid. And it helps to stay calm and breathe deeply."

Annabelle noticed several of the dolls glancing at one another. Tiffany looked down at her shoes.

"All right," said Auntie Sarah, "that's fine, but is there anything you think we should do about *Mimi*?"

"Well . . . well . . ." The dolls waited. "I think . . . that . . . we should do nothing," Annabelle answered finally.

"Nothing?" said Uncle Doll.

"Not exactly *nothing*," replied Annabelle. "What I mean is that I think if we leave Mimi alone, eventually she'll get herself in big trouble. She'll do herself in.

"We should go back to our regular lives," Annabelle continued, remembering the nerve-racking walk through the hall to Nora's room and back. She did not want to feel that way anymore. "We can choose not to be afraid," she said. "And that's what we have to do. We have to be on the alert, of course. We have to keep our eyes open for whatever trouble Mimi might cause. But I think that what matters is

197

that we are positive and Mimi is negative, and in the end our positive actions will win out over Mimi's negative ones. Why poke a stick in a hornet's nest?"

There was another moment of silence. This was followed by shuffling of feet and more glances and plenty of raised eyebrows. At last Uncle Doll said, "That's all well and good, Annabelle, but meanwhile there is a monster in our midst. Do you really think all we need to do is take deep breaths?"

"Yeah, the monster is trying to bowl us over with cat toys, and we're just supposed to breathe and think nice thoughts?" said Bailey.

"Well . . ." Annabelle remembered the chaos at BJ's house. She remembered the barricades and traps and spying and plans. What had all that led to? Torn posters and nicks in the bed and missing dolls. Still, when Annabelle looked around at the faces of her family and her friends, she felt like a balloon with the air seeping out of it.

CHAPTER FIFTEEN

The Captain Comes Back

Y OU KNOW something, Annabelle," said Tiffany, moving closer to her friend. "I think that's a very interesting idea. I really do." Tiffany glared around at the other dolls.

"Why, Tiffany is right, of course," said Mama Doll after a moment. "Yes, Annabelle, you've come up with a most interesting idea. You never know what positive thinking might accomplish."

"It can't hurt," said Dad Funcraft.

"We'll certainly try to incorporate it into our plan," said Auntie Sarah.

Annabelle didn't answer them. She edged away from Tiffany and sat quietly apart from the others while they discussed plans for trapping Mean Mimi. She knew her friends and family were just being nice to her. They probably even felt sorry for her. Well, thought Annabelle, then they could go ahead and feel sorry. That was their problem, not hers.

The Dolls and the Funcrafts didn't end the meeting of the NDA until it was nearly time for the Palmers to wake up. Dad Funcraft, Bailey, and Baby Britney were about to return to Nora's room when Tiffany said, "Hey! We never decided where Annabelle and I should go. Where do you think Kate and Nora would expect to find us?"

"They didn't notice us after we came back yesterday," said Annabelle, "but I guess we should return to where they had left us before we went on the Exploration with Auntie Sarah."

"Yes, that sounds safest," agreed Papa.

So the Funcrafts hurried off, except for Mom, who was one of the heap on the parlor floor of the Dolls' house. Annabelle, many days earlier (a lifetime earlier, she thought), had been sitting awkwardly in the kitchen before she left on the Exploration with Auntie Sarah. Now she returned to her spot. And she began to worry. She had a long list of things to worry about—whether the Funcrafts would reach their home safely, whether Kate would notice that Annabelle had been missing and then had mysteriously returned, whether Mean Mimi had been hiding in Kate's room and had overheard the discussions of the NDA. And then she remembered her plan— positive thinking and deep breathing. She set her worries aside and instead imagined the Funcrafts walking calmly through the hallway, encountering no one, and quietly entering their home while Nora slept on. Then she imagined Kate waking and going about her morning without so much as a glance at the dollhouse. She tried to imagine Mimi somewhere in the Palmers' house, far from Kate's room, but she didn't want to think about what Mimi might be doing, so she practiced her deep breathing instead.

Breathe in, breathe out. Calm, calm, calm.

Several hours later the last of the Palmers had left for school or work or errands, and Annabelle heard only empty-house noises. She glanced into the parlor and called softly, "Papa? Can we move about now?"

"Papa? Can we move about now?" a singsong voice mimicked from below.

Without waiting for permission, Annabelle leapt from her chair and leaned over the edge of the dollhouse.

"Who said that?" Auntie Sarah demanded to know. She peered down from her bedroom.

"Who said that?" repeated the voice.

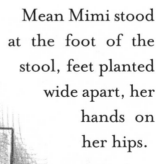

Mean Mimi stood at the foot of the stool, feet planted wide apart, her hands on her hips.

"Is that you, Mimi?" called Papa Doll.

"Is that you, Mimi?" called Mimi.

"Young lady, I don't care for that behavior," said Nanny.

"Young lady, I don't care for that behavior," said Mean Mimi. She grinned.

"Stop that this instant!" cried Uncle Doll.

"Stop that this instant!" cried Mimi.

Bobby joined Annabelle at the edge of the dollhouse. "I'm a whiny little toad!" he shouted.

"I'm a whiny little toad!" said Mean Mimi.

"See? She admits it!" Bobby exclaimed triumphantly. "She's a whiny toad and she admits it."

Annabelle began to laugh. "You're the one true Queen of All Dolls, Annabelle!" she yelled. She smiled down at Mimi, waiting.

Mimi marched huffily out of the room.

"You can't even play your own game!" Bobby called after her.

Several minutes later Tiffany and Bailey peeked into Kate's room. "Is the coast clear?" Bailey called softly.

"All clear! Come on up!" replied Bobby.

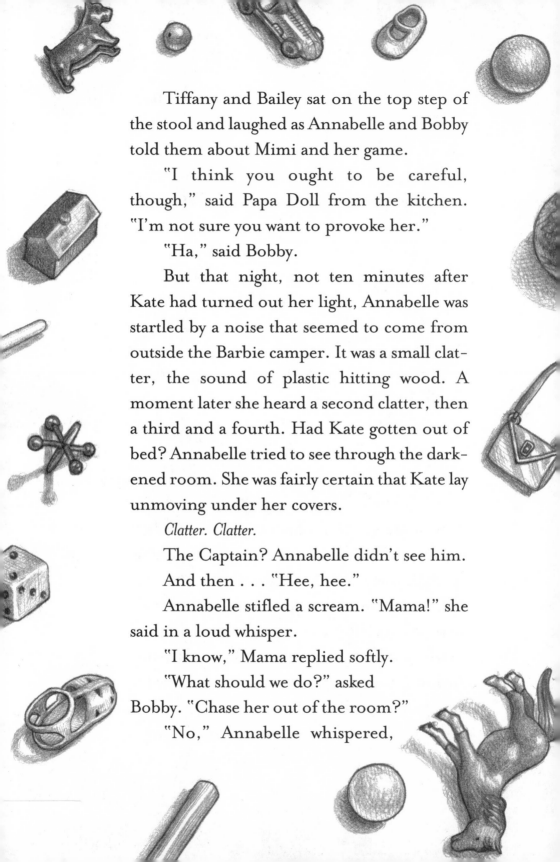

Tiffany and Bailey sat on the top step of the stool and laughed as Annabelle and Bobby told them about Mimi and her game.

"I think you ought to be careful, though," said Papa Doll from the kitchen. "I'm not sure you want to provoke her."

"Ha," said Bobby.

But that night, not ten minutes after Kate had turned out her light, Annabelle was startled by a noise that seemed to come from outside the Barbie camper. It was a small clatter, the sound of plastic hitting wood. A moment later she heard a second clatter, then a third and a fourth. Had Kate gotten out of bed? Annabelle tried to see through the darkened room. She was fairly certain that Kate lay unmoving under her covers.

Clatter. Clatter.

The Captain? Annabelle didn't see him. And then . . . "Hee, hee."

Annabelle stifled a scream. "Mama!" she said in a loud whisper.

"I know," Mama replied softly.

"What should we do?" asked Bobby. "Chase her out of the room?"

"No," Annabelle whispered,

remembering her plan. "Don't do anything."

"But she's going to wake Kate up!" Nanny hissed.

"And if Kate wakes up, she'll see that we're all exactly where she left us," replied Annabelle.

"But what is she going to think about this strange doll who's running around her room?" asked Uncle Doll. Annabelle could see that he was twisting his hands.

"Well . . ." said Annabelle.

"Rumors," said Papa Doll with a small moan. "This is how they start. And they spread quickly."

Despite herself, a chill ran through Annabelle.

The next morning, Kate's floor was awash in tiny toys—old Barbie accessories, jacks, pieces from a game of Monopoly, a plastic horse, Mr. Potato Head's eyes. Annabelle watched nervously as Kate woke up and sat on the edge of her bed. She rubbed her eyes. She yawned. And then she looked at the floor. Frowning, she leaned over and fingered the plastic horse. She dropped it and reached for a

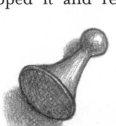

Barbie purse. Then, still frowning, she gathered up all the toys and set them in a pile on her desk.

"Nora!" she called.

Annabelle breathed a sigh of relief. But she wondered how long Kate would be able to blame Nora for Mimi's messes.

That night, the NDA met again.

"This has become urgent," said Auntie Sarah. "We must trap Mimi quickly."

"Why not trap her right in the camper?" suggested Papa. "That would be efficient. Trap her there and keep her there."

The dolls agreed that this was a good idea,

and for the rest of that night and the one after that, they worked on a plan.

Mimi was busy too. On the first night, she tried to set up a missile launch in Nora's room like the one she'd built at BJ's house. But she couldn't find enough pieces of track. In the morning Nora discovered four pieces of railway track and six small cars on her floor, and called her mother in to look at them. Mrs. Palmer scratched her head, and the Funcrafts held their breaths.

The next night, while the dolls finalized their plan, Mimi located an old action figure at the bottom of Kate's toy chest and tried to order it around, but it stared vacantly at the wall. She left it sitting on top of the chest and Kate shrieked when she saw it the next morning.

"Our plan goes into action immed- iately," said Papa Doll the moment the Palmers had left the house. "Quickly now! Get to work."

Annabelle ran to Nora's room to alert the Funcrafts. Then, working swiftly and qui- etly (since they didn't know where Mean Mimi might be lurking), the dolls opened the door

to
the Barbie
camper and tied
one end of a length of string
to the handle. They fastened the
other end to the leg of Kate's desk. A pink
shoelace, nearly invisible against the pink
camper, was tied to a latch at the bottom of the
open door, and a bell was attached to it.

"And now for the best part," said Tiffany.
"The lure." Tiffany placed a sparkly silver
doll's tiara in the doorway of the camper. She
had found it under Nora's bed. "Mean Mimi
won't be able to resist this," she exclaimed.
"Another crown. It's perfect for a princess,
perfect for a queen."

"All right," said Dad Funcraft. "This is
serious. Let's be sure we know what we're

208

supposed to do. We haven't got much time. Not if we want to trap Mimi before Grandma Katherine comes back. She'll be the first one home."

As usual, Auntie Sarah took over. "Mrs. Funcraft," she said, "you hide somewhere near the camper. The rest of us will hide in Kate's room, except for Annabelle and Tiffany. You two call Mimi. Taunt her, tease her, do whatever is necessary to get her to come into the room—but don't let her see you. When she spots the tiara she'll enter the camper, tripping over the shoelace, which will make the bell ring. As soon as you hear the bell," Auntie Sarah continued, looking at Mom Funcraft, "cut the string. The door will slam shut, and we'll help you fasten the latches. Mimi will be trapped inside."

"But what if she makes noise?" asked Nanny nervously. "What if she bangs around inside the camper while Kate is in her room? What if—"

"We can't think about the what-ifs just now," replied Auntie Sarah. "We have agreed that we must trap her. So let's trap her. Come on. Time's a-wasting."

209

The dolls took their places. Annabelle and Tiffany stood in Kate's doorway. Annabelle called, "Mimi! Oh, Mimi! Where are you?

And Tiffany shouted, "Come and get us, Mean Mimi! Come and—"

"Tiffany! I think I hear something!" cried Annabelle. "I do! I hear footsteps! Hide!"

Annabelle and Tiffany ducked back into Kate's room and slid under her dresser. The footsteps grew louder. In a matter of seconds the bell rang. Then Annabelle heard a small bang, which she hoped was the camper door closing. And *then* she heard a great, horrid, enormous clatter, followed by an angry meow.

Annabelle peeked out from beneath the dresser and gasped when she saw The Captain, the shoelace caught on his collar, tear out of Kate's room with the camper crashing along behind him. At the same time, she heard a car door slam and knew that Grandma Katherine had come home.

"Uh-oh," said Annabelle.

CHAPTER SIXTEEN

Former Best Friends

ALARMED, Annabelle turned to look at the spot where the camper had stood. What she saw now was a dusty rectangle of bare floor amid stuffed animals, a clothes rack, and an E-Z Bake Oven. In front of a large lion stood Mom Funcraft, her mouth in a perfect *O* of surprise, one hand still clutching the string, the other clutching the tiara.

"I cut the string like I was supposed to," Mom Funcraft managed to say. "I don't know how—"

"Captain!" the dolls heard Grandma Katherine exclaim from downstairs.

"Hide! Hide! Everybody, hide!"squeaked Uncle Doll.

The Funcrafts, carrying the string and the tiara, fled from Kate's room faster than Annabelle had ever seen them run. And the Dolls scrambled up the stool to their house in less than two minutes. By the time Grandma Katherine entered Kate's room, Annabelle and her family were in their positions in the dollhouse.

Grandma Katherine carried the camper back to its spot and set it down. Annabelle was surprised to see that she looked annoyed rather than startled or puzzled. But when Grandma Katherine turned and saw The Captain pad warily into the room behind her, Annabelle understood why.

"There you are, Captain, you naughty thing," said Grandma Katherine. She scooped The Captain into her arms. "I *told* Annie you couldn't be trusted upstairs, but she wanted to give you another chance. And look what happened! You could have gotten hurt, Captain. How on earth do you get yourself into these situations?" Grandma Katherine carried The Captain down the hall, talking all the way.

Annabelle knew The Captain would once again be banished to the first floor, but she barely felt relieved. Compared to Mean Mimi, The Captain was nothing more than an annoyance—like a flea or a hiccup. Mean Mimi was another story.

Annabelle glanced at the Barbie camper. The shoelace was gone, but attached to the door handle was a tiny piece of string. It was the only sign of the Dolls' plan to capture Mimi. Annabelle told herself to be sure to remove the string that night, before Kate noticed it.

The dolls knew that they had been taking too many risks since Mean Mimi had arrived. For the next three days they stayed put in their houses, except when Annabelle ventured out to remove the string. They saw no sign of either Mean Mimi or The Captain. Annabelle hadn't expected to see The Captain again, but Mimi's disappearance made her feel nervous. On the third evening she was desperate to talk to Tiffany.

"Can I please visit Tiffany tonight?" she begged her parents. "*Please?* We can't hide in our houses forever. We'll go crazy. Plus, we don't want Mimi to think she has that kind of power over us, do we? She can't make us prisoners in our homes."

The Dolls relented more quickly than Annabelle had expected, partly because Auntie Sarah announced that she thought it was high time she began planning another Exploration. "Annabelle's right," she said. "We can't hole up endlessly."

"I can," muttered Uncle Doll, but Mama and Papa ignored him. And at last they gave Annabelle permission to visit Tiffany.

"Go straight to Nora's room, though," they admonished her. "No dilly-dallying."

Five minutes later Annabelle was hurrying through the Palmers' hallway, then picking her way among the toys on Nora's floor. "Yoo-hoo!" she called softly when she reached Tiffany's house.

Tiffany was overjoyed to see her friend. "It feels like it's been three years instead of three days," she said. "Want to go to the attic? I bet Mimi hasn't found the attic yet."

Annabelle wasn't so sure, and the thought of creeping around with Mimi on the loose terrified her, until she remembered her own words. She did not, in fact, want Mimi to think she had any power over the dolls. And so she agreed to go to the attic with Tiffany.

"Do you think it will be okay with your parents?" Tiffany wanted to know.

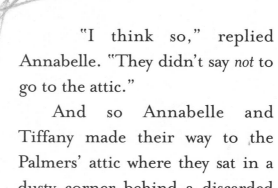

"I think so," replied Annabelle. "They didn't say *not* to go to the attic."

And so Annabelle and Tiffany made their way to the Palmers' attic where they sat in a dusty corner behind a discarded hatbox. Usually they tried to find a spot of moonlight, but not on this evening. They wanted darkness.

"Isn't it creepy?" said Tiffany when they had settled onto the floor.

"You mean that we haven't seen Mean Mimi?"

"Yes. Where do you think she is?"

Annabelle wrinkled her nose. "I don't know. The scary thing is that she could be anywhere."

"Maybe Kate or Nora found her," said Tiffany.

"Maybe
she's been closed in a
drawer or shut in a closet
and she can't get out."

"Maybe she left the Palmers' house," suggested Annabelle.

"On her *own*?" exclaimed Tiffany.

"Why not?" Annabelle tried to sound casual, but the thought of a doll walking along the street made Annabelle shiver.

"You're afraid, aren't you?" asked Tiffany.

"Yes," Annabelle admitted. "I'm trying so hard to think about positive things and to do my breathing exercises, but . . . sometimes I just can't help thinking about what trouble Mean Mimi might cause. And about what could happen if too many humans become suspicious about dolls. Rumors and all that. They really are very dangerous."

"I know," said Tiffany in a small voice.

"And then I feel vulnerable," Annabelle continued. "Auntie Sarah explained that word to me. And even though feeling vulnerable is understandable—that's what Auntie Sarah said—it isn't helpful to me, so mostly I concentrate on feeling smart and strong and positive."

A rustle nearby made Annabelle and Tiffany jump.

"What was that?" Tiffany whispered.

When they heard nothing more, Annabelle said, "Probably just a mouse."

And Tiffany agreed. "Probably," she said in a small voice.

"You know what else?" Annabelle said after a moment. "This is a negative thought and I have to tell myself to stop thinking it, but sometimes it creeps back anyway."

"What is it?" asked Tiffany.

"Well," said Annabelle, "I'm afraid that all this trouble is my fault."

"Your fault? How is it your fault?"

"Because if I hadn't fallen in the spider's web during our Exploration with Auntie Sarah then we would have come downstairs just a few minutes earlier and we wouldn't have had to hide in Kate's backpack and we wouldn't have gone off to school with her and we wouldn't have gone to BJ's house and

Mean Mimi wouldn't have come home with us."

"Oh, Annabelle," said Tiffany. "You couldn't help tripping. Besides, Auntie Sarah had already let us stay in the attic too long."

"I know. But I did trip, and it made us even later. I'm not like you, Tiffany. You do everything right. You're bold and strong and adventurous. Just like Auntie Sarah. And I'm—I'm afraid of falling and climbing. I'm even afraid of getting wet. I'm—"

"You're you, Annabelle," said Tiffany.

Annabelle managed a small smile.

* * *

Two nights later, long after the Palmers had gone to bed, Annabelle Doll sat inside the Barbie camper, practicing her breathing and enjoying having a few minutes all to herself.

Breathe in, breathe out. Calm, calm, calm.

She leaned back in a plastic chair and gazed out the window of the camper. Kate's room, bathed in moonlight, was still. She heard nothing from the dollhouse, nothing from the direction of Kate's bed.

Breathe in, breathe out. Calm, calm, calm.

SLAM.

The door of the camper banged open so fast and with such force that Annabelle, startled, slid sideways off of the chair and tumbled to the floor with a gasp.

Mean Mimi stood in the doorway, her glittery princess clothes sparkling in the moonlight. "*Bonjour*, crybaby," she greeted Annabelle.

Annabelle climbed back into the chair and sat up straight, pushing the chair as far from the door as possible. "Mimi!" she cried. She glanced out the window of the camper, but she could see only a corner of the dollhouse. "What are you doing here?"

"Well," Mimi began, idly twirling a lock of her hair, "I just thought you'd be interested to know that I heard Tiffany and your aunt talking about you last night."

"What?" Annabelle tried to back away, but could move no further.

"Yup, I heard them talking about you. And you know what? They're planning a *big*

Exploration—and they're not going to invite you along."

"They aren't?" Annabelle was surprised and confused.

"No. Because you always ruin things. Like when you fell in the spider's web."

"How did you know I fell in a spider's web?"

"I just *told* you. I heard Tiffany and your aunt talking. Tiffany said she's tired of hanging around with a 'fraidy cat. You're no fun to be with. You're afraid of everything. What a bore. Plus," Mimi continued with a sweet smile, "you're the cause of everyone's problems, because if it weren't for you, *I* wouldn't be here."

Annabelle tried to speak, but could think of nothing to say. She had confided these fears in only one person. Tiffany. And Tiffany had betrayed her.

"Well," said Mimi, "just thought I'd drop by for a chat. See you later."

Annabelle watched Mimi run through Kate's room and disappear into the hallway. She sat very still for a moment. She wanted to talk to someone, but the two people with

whom she ordinarily shared her problems
were Tiffany and Auntie Sarah. And she was
never, ever going to talk to either one of them
again. Ever.

Annabelle stood up and looked out the
camper door. Where were Tiffany and Auntie
Sarah anyway? She hadn't seen them in several hours. Were they already on the
Exploration? Without her?

Annabelle decided she was going to sit in
the doorway of the camper until she saw
Tiffany, and then she was going to ask her a
few questions. So Annabelle sat. And sat. And
sat. And the longer she sat, the more cross
she felt.

It was just before dawn when Annabelle
saw Tiffany peek into Kate's room. Tiffany
was alone—no Auntie Sarah—and Annabelle
was glad. "Tiffany!" she called softly.

"Oh, hi! There you are!" Tiffany replied,
and she hurried across the room and stood
outside the camper. "What have you been up
to tonight?"

"Do you care?" replied Annabelle.

"What?"

"I said, 'Do you care?'"

"I know that's what you said, but what's it supposed to mean?"

"It means when I tell you secrets I don't expect you to tell them to anyone else."

"Annabelle, I don't know what you're talking about."

"Oh, no?" Annabelle, one hand on her hip, told Tiffany about Mean Mimi's visit.

"But I didn't say anything to anyone!" cried Tiffany. "I swear. I didn't say a word."

"Then how come Mimi knows about the spider's web and everything? You're the only one I said those things to."

"Well, that's not my problem," replied Tiffany.

"You sound awfully defensive," said Annabelle.

"I sound defensive because my best friend is accusing me of talking behind her back." Tiffany paused. "Excuse me, my *former* best friend."

"Well, excuse *me*, I don't have a best friend, former or otherwise, so don't worry about it."

"Fine, I won't worry about it. And anyway, I'm not speaking to you."

"Well, I'm not speaking to you!" cried Annabelle.

"Fine."

"Fine."

Tiffany marched back across Kate's room and into the night. And Annabelle, feeling more miserable than she had ever felt in her whole long life, marched into the dollhouse and got into her bed. She pulled the covers over her head, then called, "And don't anybody try to talk to me!"

CHAPTER SEVENTEEN

Mean Mimi Meets Her End

ANNABELLE didn't speak to Tiffany for an entire week. And she spoke as little as possible to Auntie Sarah. She had intended not to speak to her at all, but living in such close quarters made that difficult. Anyway, Annabelle was angrier with Tiffany than with Auntie Sarah. She understood why Auntie Sarah might not want her to go along on Explorations. She was disappointed, but she understood. Tiffany, however, had betrayed Annabelle. Annabelle did not understand that, and she thought it was unforgivable.

That long, lonely week was even worse for Annabelle than the many years before she had had a best friend. No best friend at all was better than a best friend who had become a traitor. Annabelle spent hours lying on her bed, thinking and remembering. She remembered the first time she had met Tiffany, when the Funcrafts and their dream house had been delivered to the Palmers in a large cardboard carton. She remembered reading Auntie Sarah's diary with Tiffany, and forming SELMP. She remembered when Tiffany told her that if she had a friendship necklace, she would share it with Annabelle.

Ha, thought Annabelle. If I had that necklace now I'd give it back to Tiffany—after

227

I had scratched TRAITOR on her half of the heart. BEST TRAITOR.

During this miserable week, Annabelle kept track of the times Mean Mimi was spotted in Kate's room. Four visits in all—once to call to Kate again while she slept, once to make another nighttime mess on the floor of Kate's room, once to deposit a cat toy in the Dolls' parlor (they managed to hide it before Kate noticed it), and once to announce to Annabelle that she, Princess Mimi, was Tiffany Funcraft's new best friend.

The Dolls grew afraid that their secret life might be exposed at any moment, and that they would be able to do nothing about it.

"Good idea, Annabelle," said Bobby crossly one night. "Doing nothing about Mean Mimi is working just great."

Annabelle felt equally cross. "As if trapping her was such a good idea," she replied.

"Children," Auntie Sarah called softly from her room. "Please."

"Oh, be quiet," muttered Annabelle, but not so that anyone could hear her.

That was on a Monday night. On Tuesday night, there was no sign of Mimi. She's probably in Nora's room, torturing the Funcrafts, thought Annabelle. Or maybe she's whispering with Tiffany, her new best friend. But on Wednesday night there was no sign of Mimi either. Nor on Thursday night, nor on Friday night.

"Do you suppose maybe she's gone?" ventured Papa after Kate had fallen asleep. "Do you think she left? Perhaps for good?"

"It's possible," replied Mama. "I guess anything is possible."

"How could she leave?" asked Nanny.

Annabelle thought of her conversation in the attic with Tiffany, of the idea of Mimi walking boldly down a street in the big outside world of the humans. She didn't want to frighten her family, though, so she said, "Maybe she decided to go back to BJ's house. Maybe she decided she punished Tiffany and me enough, and she left for school in Kate's backpack."

"Punished you?" repeated Auntie Sarah.

Annabelle wouldn't look at her aunt, but she said, "Yes. We ruined her life at BJ's. I think maybe she followed us here to teach us a lesson but didn't plan to stay."

Annabelle's family looked both hopeful and thoughtful.

"That would mean," said Mama, "that she's making life miserable again for Callie's dolls."

"Maybe and maybe not," Annabelle answered. "She doesn't have much control over them anymore." But Annabelle knew that Mean Mimi could still be dangerous to dolls everywhere.

"Perhaps," said Uncle Doll, "our lives can return to normal now."

Saturday afternoon was raw and rainy with an autumn wind that whistled around the corners of the Palmers' house, rattling the windows and creeping through cracks. Kate closed herself into her room, curled up on her bed, covered herself with a blanket, and began to read *Half Magic*.

Ordinarily, Annabelle would have enjoyed a day like this—all cozy and quiet, with Kate nearby. But Nora had secretly played in the Dolls' house that morning, and she had

left Tiffany and her par-
ents in the parlor with
Annabelle. Mom and Dad
Funcraft were lying on the
floor. Annabelle and
Tiffany were sitting
jammed together in an
armchair. Each had
quietly pinched the
other five times
already. And before
Kate had entered the
room, Annabelle
had whispered to Tiffany, "Traitor!" and
Tiffany had replied, "Liar!"

Now Annabelle could neither pinch nor
whisper, not with Kate so close at hand. But
she could feel anger bubbling inside her, and
imagined she could feel Tiffany's anger bubbling as well.

Annabelle tried to concentrate on Kate.
She wished Nora would come into the room
so that Kate would read aloud to her. Then
she wished that Kate would leave so that
Annabelle could pinch Tiffany again. Then
she forgot about Kate and began a list of

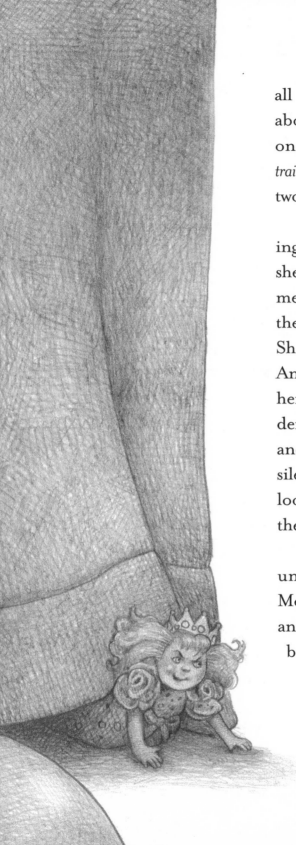

all the things she hated about Tiffany. Number one on the list was, *She's a traitor.* So were numbers two and three.

Annabelle was working on number four when she thought she saw movement on the floor near the head of Kate's bed. She glanced to the left. And what she saw made her eyes widen. She wondered if Tiffany saw it too, and she tried to send a silent message to her to look to the left, look to the left.

Creeping out from under Kate's bed was Mean Mimi. She paused and peered up—up at the bedspread hanging over the side. Then she crossed the room to Kate's bookcase;

just ran through the room with Kate lying right there on the bed.

Annabelle couldn't stand it any longer. She was going to have to break a teeny little rule herself. She wanted to make sure she wasn't the only person watching what was going on. So she nudged Tiffany and twisted slightly to look at her. Tiffany gave Annabelle the smallest of nods. Then, as the girls turned their attention back to Mimi, Tiffany slid her hand into Annabelle's. And that is how they sat and watched the most frightening and most amazing thing either of them had ever seen or has ever seen since.

Mimi ran to Kate's bookcase and began to climb up it. She was no more than ten feet in front of Kate. If Kate had so much as glanced up from *Half Magic,* she would have seen a small doll in a princess costume climbing swiftly up her bookcase, using the books themselves as stepping-stones toward the top.

Please don't look up, don't look up, Kate, Annabelle chanted silently, and she felt Tiffany's grip tighten around her hand.

When Mimi reached the fourth shelf

from the bottom, she turned around
and stood on a paperback book that
was lying on its side—stood and
faced Kate Palmer.

"Kate!" Mimi called, and
Annabelle cringed to hear how loudly
Mimi could shout.

Kate heard her, which didn't surprise
Annabelle, but scared her nevertheless, and as
Kate looked up from her book, two things
happened at the very same time: Mean Mimi
leapt from the shelf, and the door to Kate's
room was flung open as Nora entered.

Kate turned around to glare at Nora and
said sternly, "Nora, how many times have I
told you to knock first?"

But Nora only pointed at Mean Mimi
and screamed, "That dolly! She jumped off
your bookshelf! I saw her! I saw her!"

Kate looked at the floor where Mean
Mimi was now lying motionless, eyes staring
blankly at the ceiling. "Oh, Nora," she said.
"She couldn't have *jumped*. She must have
fallen somehow."

Annabelle knew that Kate hadn't actually
seen Mimi jump. She had heard someone call

her name, and then Nora had burst into her
room. Still, Kate slid off of her bed very
slowly, and when she bent to examine Mean
Mimi, she was frowning.

2 3 5

"She jumped! She jumped!" Nora was crying.

"She couldn't have," Kate repeated. But she picked Mimi up gingerly, holding the edge of her sleeve between her thumb and forefinger.

"She did! I *saw* her!"

"Nora, stop that," said Kate, but Annabelle thought she sounded nervous rather than cross. "Please be quiet."

Nora stopped talking. She sniffled and wiped her eyes with the back of her hand.

"Whose doll is this, anyway?" asked Kate, still allowing Mimi to dangle from her fingers.

"I don't know," replied Nora, who sounded as if she might start to cry again. "I don't have a princess doll."

Kate dropped Mimi on her desk, and led Nora to the bed. "Don't worry about it," she said kindly. "Here. Look at this book. I just started it. It's all about magic, and it's really good. I'll read to you for a while."

Kate and Nora sat together on the bed for a long time. Annabelle didn't take her eyes off Mimi. She barely even listened to the story. But although she stared at Mimi for half an hour while Kate read to Nora, and then for another three hours as the afternoon dragged on, she didn't see Mimi so much as blink.

Annabelle stared at Mimi while the Palmers ate their dinner downstairs. She stared at her during the stormy fall evening while the Palmers talked on the phone and watched television and Kate and Nora took their baths and got ready for bed.

Kate had been asleep for a full hour when Annabelle dared to stir. She turned to Tiffany and whispered, "I haven't seen Mimi move. Have you?"

"Nope."

Slowly the rest of the Dolls joined Annabelle and Tiffany and Mom and Dad Funcraft in the parlor. They stared down at Mimi. Several of them had seen her jump. Those who hadn't had listened to Kate and Nora, and figured out some of what had happened. Annabelle and Tiffany filled them in on the rest.

"And she hasn't moved since Nora saw her land on the floor," Annabelle said at last. "She's definitely in Doll State."

Uncle Doll said thoughtfully, "Could anyone see Kate's clock when Mimi jumped?"

"I could," said Tiffany. "It was about two-thirty."

"All right," said Uncle Doll. "We'll see what happens at two-thirty tomorrow afternoon. I hope she doesn't do anything foolish when she's released from Doll State."

Kate did not move Mimi from her desk. All the next day Annabelle watched both Mimi and the clock. She expected just about anything to happen at two-thirty, especially since the Palmers had decided to spend the day

across town with Kate and Nora's cousins, so the house was empty of humans.

The very last thing Annabelle expected Mimi to do was nothing. But that was what happened at two-thirty. Nothing.

"Are you sure Kate's clock said two-thirty yesterday?" Uncle Doll asked Tiffany.

"Positive."

The dolls watched Mimi for another hour and still nothing happened. She lay on Kate's desk in the position in which Kate had dropped her—an arm flung over her head, one leg across the other. When Kate went to bed that night, Mimi continued to lie motionless on the desk. She was still there in the morning.

As soon as the Palmers had left the house, the Dolls and Tiffany and her parents once again gathered in the parlor and regarded Mimi.

"What do you think?" asked Annabelle in an awed whisper. "It's been lots longer than twenty-four hours."

"She hasn't moved a muscle," said Auntie Sarah softly.

"Maybe she got hurt when she jumped off the shelf," said Bobby.

"She doesn't look hurt," replied Mama. "I don't see any cracks. She's all in one piece."

After this the dolls were quiet for a very long time. Finally Annabelle decided to say the scary thing she'd been thinking. "Do you suppose she could be in PDS?"

Nanny gasped and her hand flew to her mouth.

Annabelle glanced at Tiffany. The girls were talking to one another again, but in a cautious way, because they had not yet discussed their fight.

"PDS," said Tiffany in a tiny voice. "I don't know. . . . How can you tell if someone's in PDS?"

"Let's go poke her," said Bobby, brightening.

"Bobby!" admonished Nanny.

"Well, someone has to take a look at her," he said.

Reluctantly, the grown-ups agreed, and

in the end everyone except Nanny and Baby Betsy made their way across Kate's room to her bed, and finally onto her desk. They tiptoed through the scattered pencils and markers, a Slinky, and three china cats, and then they were standing over Mean Mimi.

For a moment, they merely stared at her. Then Annabelle stuck her foot out and poked Mimi's head with the toe of her shoe.

Nothing.

Tiffany, feeling braver, leaned over and shook Mimi's shoulder.

Nothing.

"Mimi! Wake up!" yelled Bobby.

Nothing.

"Is this PDS?" asked Tiffany.

"I suppose it must be," replied Auntie Sarah.

"So it's real," whispered Annabelle. "It's really real." She looked at her aunt's solemn face and felt as if a chilly wind were blowing through the bedroom.

"I guess this is good for the dolls at BJ's house," she said after a while.

"I guess," agreed Tiffany, looking shaken.

"What do you think we should do about her?" asked Mom Funcraft.

"I'm afraid we can do nothing," replied Auntie Sarah. "We have to leave her right here where Kate put her."

And there Mimi lay for two more days, in full view of the dolls, an uncomfortable reminder of things they did not yet understand.

CHAPTER EIGHTEEN

Home Sweet Home, Once Again

ON THURSDAY morning Annabelle attempted something for which she had not had the courage in quite sometime: she left the dollhouse, walked down the Palmers' hallway to Nora's room, and knocked on the Funcrafts' front door. The Captain was again banished to the first floor, and Mimi continued to lie unmoving on Kate's desk, so Annabelle felt safe for the first time in a very long time. Her heart was heavy, though, and she knew she wouldn't feel better until she and Tiffany had talked about their fight.

"Hi,
Annabelle!"
Tiffany greeted her.

"Hi," Annabelle
replied. "Tiffany, we need to
talk. Can we go somewhere private?"

Tiffany looked around Nora's room.
"How about the shoe box in the closet?"
she suggested.

So Annabelle and Tiffany sat in the
empty shoe box, which was lying on its side at
the back of Nora's closet.

"We need to talk, don't you think?" said
Annabelle a bit nervously.

"About Mimi?" asked Tiffany.

"No, about our fight."

Tiffany poked at her shoe. "Yeah. I knew that was what you meant."

Annabelle drew in a deep breath and let it out slowly. "Okay," she began. "You see, I thought we were best friends."

"I thought so too," said Tiffany.

"Then why did you tell Mean Mimi all those private things I told you? I know I didn't *say* not to tell them to anybody, but I thought you would understand that."

"But, Annabelle, I didn't tell Mimi anything. I barely even talked to her."

"Then how did she know that I fell in the spider's web on the Exploration with you and Auntie Sarah? And how did she know that I think I always ruin things?"

Tiffany shook her head.

"I only said those things once—the night you and I snuck up to the attic to talk."

Tiffany had been frowning, but now her eyes widened. "Oh! Oh!" she cried. "Annabelle!"

"What?"

"Remember when we heard that noise and we thought maybe it was a mouse? I bet it was Mimi! I bet she was up in the attic eavesdropping on our conversation. *And*," Tiffany continued, "I bet the mouse we thought we heard at BJ's was Mimi crawling into the backpack."

"Oh, ew!" exclaimed Annabelle. And then, "Mimi was so sneaky. She was—she was devious. Those other things she said—about you and Auntie Sarah planning an Exploration without me—"

"We never planned an Exploration without you."

"Mimi said you did, though. She also said that you said I wasn't fun to be around. That I'm boring, and you were tired of hanging around with a 'fraidy cat. I guess she just made those things up."

"Of course she did!" exclaimed Tiffany. "I would never say anything like that about you. Don't you know that, Annabelle? You really are my best friend." Tiffany paused and looked thoughtfully at Annabelle. "How could you believe such things?"

"I guess," Annabelle answered, "because those are the things I worry about. They're the things *I'm* afraid might be true. I wonder how

Mimi knew all that. She certainly was smart, for such a horrible doll. Tiffany, I'm sorry I didn't believe you. And I'm sorry I called you a traitor."

"And I'm sorry I called you a liar and said you were my former best friend. You'll *always* be my best friend."

"And you'll always be mine," replied Annabelle.

By the time Kate returned from school that afternoon, Annabelle and the Dolls were in the places in which Kate had left them the night before when she had tidied up the doll-house. Annabelle was propped against the end of her bed, looking out into Kate's room.

So she had a good view of things when Kate delicately picked up Mimi, studied her, and then called, "Grandma Katherine?"

A moment or two later, Grandma Katherine appeared in Kate's doorway. Kate held Mimi out to her and said, "Look what I found in my room last weekend. I don't know who she belongs to. She isn't Nora's, and I asked at school, and she isn't Harmoni's or Ayanna's or Rachel's. Nora asked Martha, and she doesn't belong to her either."

"Hmm," said Grandma Katherine. "That's strange. You have no idea how she got in your room?"

Kate shook her head. "Suddenly she was just lying on my floor. Nora thought she saw her jump off my bookcase," she added.

Grandma Katherine frowned, but all she said was, "Well, I suppose you should take her to the Lost and Found at school. That seems like the best thing to do."

"Okay," agreed Kate. "I'm sure she belongs to one of Nora's friends."

On Friday morning Kate stuffed Mean Mimi in her backpack and took her to school. When she returned that afternoon, she reported to Grandma Katherine that she had left the doll in the Lost and Found bin.

"Tiffany?" said Annabelle late that night as they played in the nursery of the Dolls' house. "I had a horrible thought today."

Tiffany put down the alphabet block she'd been tossing from hand to hand. "What was it?" she asked.

"Well, I was just wondering . . . what if

Mean Mimi was pretending? What if she was fooling us and she isn't in PDS at all? I mean, what if she's still alive?"

"Aughhh!" Tiffany shrieked softly. "Annabelle, that really is a horrible thought!"

"I know."

"Well, we can't do anything about it."

Breathe in, breathe out. "The truth is," Annabelle said after a moment, "she probably *is* in PDS. That makes the most sense."

"Yes," agreed Tiffany, "it does."

"Tiffany? Do you think about the dolls at BJ's house very often?"

"Every day."

"I wonder what they're thinking now."

"What do you mean?"

"I wonder what they think happened to Mean Mimi. After all, she's been gone for a long time. And as far as they know, she just disappeared. I'm sure she didn't tell anyone what she was going to do. So all Waterfall and the others knew was that suddenly Mean Mimi wasn't around anymore. Do they think she's hiding now? Do they think Callie lost her somewhere?"

"I don't know," replied Tiffany, "but I

bet they're feeling pretty comfortable. I bet they think she's gone for good."

Annabelle smiled. "I hope so. *We* know she's in the Lost and Found, and Callie won't think to look for her there, because she didn't take Mimi to school."

"You know who I've been wondering about?" asked Tiffany.

"Who?"

"Techno-Man."

"Techno-Man! Why?"

"I feel bad for him."

"But he was evil!" said Annabelle.

"No, he wasn't. Not really. He just had to act tough for Mimi. And you saw what happened when his helmet came off. He was embarrassed. It was like he'd been lying to everyone and suddenly he was caught in his lie. But I don't think he's a bad doll. And I bet he got back in the bucket of action figures before BJ came home. I wonder if he's made friends with the other dolls yet, though."

Annabelle shook her head slowly. "I don't know." She traced the letter *S* on one of the blocks. "You know what the sad thing is? No matter what happened to Mean Mimi, she probably thought she didn't deserve it."

"If she's in PDS, she can't think any-thing," pointed out Tiffany.

"Well, no. But before that, before she jumped off the shelf. I'm talking about all her life—when she was here at the Palmers' and everyone realized how mean she was and we tried to trap her and everything. And before that, when she was at BJ's and she kept doing things to make the other dolls mad at her. It seems like no matter what she did or how people reacted to her, she still thought she was better than everyone, that she was right and they were wrong—and that every-one was mean to her. Didn't she ever under-stand?"

"Maybe not," said Tiffany. "Remember Francine? Even after Ms. Feldman caught her teasing Kate and reminded her of the class rules and made her apologize, Francine was still mean—as if it was Kate's fault that Francine had gotten in trouble."

Annabelle sighed. "I guess that's the way it is with bullies. They never learn."

"Maybe not with all bullies. Maybe just some," said Tiffany. "You know what?

I just realized that your idea worked, Annabelle."

"What?"

"Remember, you suggested that we do nothing about Mimi? You said not to poke a stick in a hornet's nest, and that if we left her alone she would get into big trouble and do *herself* in. And that's exactly what happened."

Annabelle smiled.

"How did you know that's what would happen?"

"I—I—"

"Because Annabelle is a thinker," said Auntie Sarah from her room. "I'm sorry, girls. I couldn't help overhearing your conversation."

"That's okay," said Annabelle.

"Come downstairs," Auntie Sarah called. "It's time for a talk."

"Another talk?" Tiffany whispered to Annabelle with a small groan.

"I think this one will be more pleasant than the one about our fight," Annabelle whispered back.

Annabelle and Tiffany followed Auntie Sarah all the way downstairs to the parlor

where the rest of the Dolls were gathered.

"We need a family meeting," announced Auntie Sarah.

"Can I come to a Doll family meeting?" asked Tiffany.

"You're part of the family," Mama replied, and Tiffany grinned.

"I want to say," Auntie Sarah began when everyone had settled down, "that I believe we owe Annabelle a thank-you and an apology."

"For what?" asked Bobby.

"A thank-you for showing us a wise way in which to deal with a menace. And an apology for not putting more faith in her ideas. Annabelle was exactly right about Mimi. And I think we should recognize that. Annabelle, I know sometimes you worry that you're not as daring as Tiffany."

"Or you," added Annabelle.

"Or me. Or as brave as Bobby," Auntie Sarah continued.

"Or the Funcrafts," added Annabelle.

"Or the Funcrafts. But you have other strengths. You have a good brain, and you put it to good use."

"You have a good heart," said Papa.

"Yechh," said Bobby, but he smiled at his sister.

"And you're a very good friend," said Tiffany. "Even if we fight sometimes."

"All friends fight sometimes," said Uncle Doll.

Annabelle went to bed that night thinking warm thoughts about friendship and her good brain and heart. The warm thoughts stayed with her the next morning while she lay stiffly in the dollhouse as Kate got dressed. This was often Annabelle's worry time, and today she was tempted to worry about what might happen if Mean Mimi weren't in PDS after all; if she had been doing a very good job of faking and might one day return to the Palmers' house in Kate's backpack. But she reminded her good brain to think positively.

The warm thoughts were still with her later in the morning when the Palmers' house was quiet, and Auntie Sarah said she thought it was high time she returned to the attic to begin work on her spider farm. "Now that the menace is gone," she added. "Does anyone want to come with me?"

"I bet Tiffany will," said Annabelle.

"And you?" asked Auntie Sarah.

Annabelle thought for a moment. "Well, I'm still afraid of spiders," she admitted finally, "but I do have an idea about how to harvest their silk."

"Wonderful!" said Auntie Sarah, clapping her hands together. "You may show us tonight."

But that evening, before Annabelle had a chance to show off her idea, Nora snagged her and Tiffany and Bailey and plopped them down on the floor of the bathroom. "Time for Miami Beach-a-go-go," she said.

Nora was once again dressed in her bathing suit and goggles and flippers. She ran water in the bathtub and tossed the Funcrafts into the small waves. Then she placed Annabelle in the soap dish. "You can be the

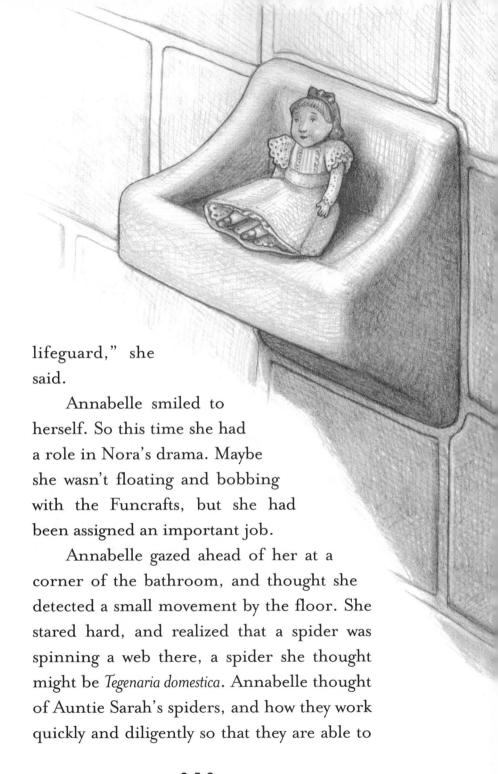

lifeguard," she
said.

Annabelle smiled to
herself. So this time she had
a role in Nora's drama. Maybe
she wasn't floating and bobbing
with the Funcrafts, but she had
been assigned an important job.

Annabelle gazed ahead of her at a
corner of the bathroom, and thought she
detected a small movement by the floor. She
stared hard, and realized that a spider was
spinning a web there, a spider she thought
might be *Tegenaria domestica*. Annabelle thought
of Auntie Sarah's spiders, and how they work
quickly and diligently so that they are able to

spin web after web. Spiders are tenacious, Annabelle realized. They start new webs, and work and work, and if the webs are damaged or destroyed, they simply repair them. I'm tenacious too, thought Annabelle. And diligent. I watch and I wait, and my good brain and I are tenacious and diligent, like spiders.

Annabelle, in her spot in the soap dish, made a list in her head: *tenacious, diligent, a good brain, a good heart, a good friend*. Then she added: *a family who loves me, good friends in return*.

There was nothing boring about any of that.

Th

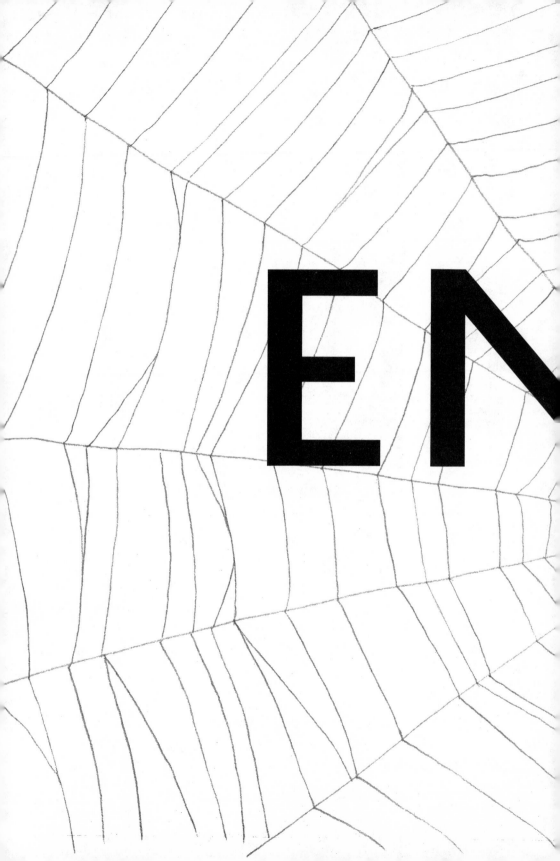

Ann M. Martin is the author of the Newbery Honor Book *A Corner of the Universe*, as well as many other books for young readers, including, with Laura Godwin, *The Doll People*; *P.S. Longer Letter Later* and *Snail Mail No More*, co-written with Paula Danziger; and *Belle Teal*. Ms. Martin funds such charities as The Lisa Libraries and The Ann M. Martin Foundation. She makes her home in upstate New York.

Laura Godwin, also known as Nola Buck, is the co-author of *The Doll People* as well as the author of many popular books for children, including *Barnyard Prayers*, illustrated by Brian Selznick; *The Flower Girl*, illustrated by John Wallace; *Christmas in the Manger*, illustrated by Felicia Bond; and *Central Park Serenade*, illustrated by Barry Root. Born and raised in Alberta, Canada, she now lives in New York City.

Brian Selznick received the Caldecott Honor for *The Dinosaurs of Waterhouse Hawkins* by Barbara Kerley. He is also the illustrator of *The Doll People*; *Wingwalker* by Rosemary Wells; *Barnyard Prayers* by Laura Godwin; *Frindle* by Andrew Clements; and *Amelia and Eleanor Go for a Ride* and *When Marian Sang*, both by Pam Muñoz Ryan. He has also written and illustrated his own books, *The Boy of a Thousand Faces* and *The Houdini Box*, the latter the winner of the Texas Bluebonnet Award. Mr. Selznick lives in Brooklyn, New York.

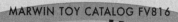

Annabelle and Tiffany's adventures begin in

The DOLL PEOPLE

CHAPTER ONE

Annabelle Doll's Secret

NNABELLE looked around the dollhouse nursery, feeling restless. "Bobby," she said to her brother, "let's play tag."

Bobby Doll was propped up in a corner by the stairway landing in the dollhouse. That was where Kate Palmer had left him before school that morning.

"Do you think that's safe, Annabelle?" asked Bobby. "The Captain is right outside."

Annabelle didn't have a chance to answer his question. "No, it's not safe!" Mama Doll called from downstairs. Mama was standing on her head next to the piano, which was where Kate had left *her* that morning. It was a most uncomfortable position. "If you move around now, Kate might come home and see you. And Bobby's right. The Captain is just outside."

Annabelle looked out the side window of the dollhouse and saw the round yellow eye of a cat staring back at her. She sighed. Why couldn't The Captain take a nap?

Annabelle flopped on her bed. She tried to remember where Kate had left her that morning. It had been somewhere in the nursery. On her bed? Sitting on the floor playing with Baby Betsy? Calling to Nanny from the doorway? Annabelle got to her feet again and peered through the window. The Captain was still standing on the shelf on which the dollhouse sat, staring in at the Dolls. When he saw Annabelle he licked his lips. Annabelle stuck her tongue out at him.

"Scat!" she called in her tiny doll voice.

"Annabelle, hush!" said Nanny.

Annabelle couldn't see Nanny, but she pushed herself away from the window anyway.

"This is so boring," she exclaimed. "My *life* is so boring."

No one answered her.

"Kate won't be home from school for ages!" she went on.

Silence.

I am going to die from boredom, thought Annabelle. She flopped on her bed again. "Mama, can I ask you a question?" she called out.

"Is it a quick question?"

"I want to know how Auntie Sarah is related to us. Is she your sister, or is she Papa's? Or is Uncle Doll your brother and—"

"Annabelle, that is not a quick question," called Papa Doll from somewhere.

And at that moment, Annabelle heard the Palmers' front door slam, heard Kate shout, "I'm home!," heard feet clattering on the stairs. The feet were somewhere near the top of the staircase when Annabelle remembered just where Kate had left her that morning. In a flash, Annabelle scooted across the nursery, and landed on Bobby's bed. By the time Kate ran into her room, Annabelle was propped against the head-board, her legs sticking out in front of her, her painted eyes staring ahead.

For the next three hours, while Kate did her third-grade homework, telephoned her friend Rachel, and tried to keep her little sister, Nora, out of her room, Annabelle sat on Bobby's bed and thought about her secret. Her secret was wonderful, and it was the only thing, the *only* thing, that prevented Annabelle from actually dying of boredom.

Annabelle recalled the moment when she had made her discovery. It had been during a night when Kate had closed the front of the dollhouse before she had gone to bed. She rarely did this, and when she did, Annabelle was delighted. It meant the Dolls had plenty of privacy during their nighttime, the time when the humans slept and the Doll family could move about their house. They could be a teeny bit less quiet, a teeny bit more free. Even The Captain, who usually snoozed at the end of Kate's bed, couldn't harm them.

And since they would have more freedom than usual on that night, Mama Doll had said, "How about a sing-along, and then free time?"

"Yes!" Annabelle had cried. Sing-alongs were always fun, and free time meant time when the Dolls could go anywhere in their house, and do anything they wanted to do, within reason. "Remember," Papa often said, "never do anything you can't *undo* by the time Kate wakes up in the morning."

The Dolls had gathered around the piano in the parlor. Uncle Doll propped two songbooks in front of him. One was a book of hymns. It had come from England a hundred years earlier with the Dolls and the house and the furniture. The other book had been purchased by Mrs. Palmer, Kate's mother, when she was a young girl and the dollhouse had been hers. On the cover of the book was a rainbow. Written across the yellow band of the rainbow were the words GREAT HITS OF THE SIXTIES.

"Let's sing 'Natural Woman,'" Annabelle had suggested.

"Yuck," said Bobby.

"Okay, then 'Respect,'" said Annabelle.

"R-E-S-P-E-C-T!" sang Bobby.

"Sockittome, sockittome, sockittome, sockittome!" Annabelle chimed in.

"How about a quieter song?" suggested Nanny.

The Dolls had sung song after song while Uncle Doll played the piano. Outside the dollhouse, Annabelle caught a glimpse of The Captain. He sat silently on Kate's bed, listening to the doll voices. He could barely hear them, but they were there, all right.

The Dolls ended the singalong after two choruses of "Bringing in the Sheaves" from the hymnbook. And then their free time began. Annabelle knew exactly what she was going to do. She wanted to examine the books in the library. And she wanted to do it privately. Lately, Kate and Rachel had talked of nothing but Nancy Drew and how she solved her mysteries. They had even read a couple of the mysteries aloud to each other, and Annabelle had listened intently. She wished she could be a detective like Nancy. And now she thought she might find something interesting on the dollhouse bookshelves. It was unlikely. But possible. Annabelle knew that most of the books on the shelves were not real. They were simply flat blocks painted bright colors, with book titles written on one side in gold ink. But perhaps she might find a secret compartment in one of the shelves. Things like that were always happening to Nancy.

So, in the glow of Kate's night-light, Annabelle had begun her search. She started by removing the books from the shelves, one by one. Presently she discovered that some of the books were attached to one another. She could remove a whole block of books at once. This was interesting, but not very mysterious. Then she discovered that some of the books were, in fact, real, like the songbooks. She could open their covers and inside were a few pages with crowded writing: *Classics of Modern Poetry, Oliver Twist*. Annabelle read the twenty-page story about the little boy named Oliver with great interest. Eagerly, she pulled out every book from the shelves. But the others were pretend. She checked for secret compartments. Nothing. She stood on a stool and tackled the next shelf. Only pretend books. She stood on tip toe and reached for the shelf above. And that was where she found Auntie Sarah's journal.

From the outside it looked like all the other books on the shelves. It was dark green, with gold writing stamped on the cover. The title was *My Journal*. It was fatter than most of the books, though, and contained dozens of pages as thin as onionskin, filled with spidery black handwriting and even some drawings.

Annabelle stepped off of the stool and sat on the floor to look through *My Journal*. She opened to the first page. And there she found the words "The Private Diary of Sarah Doll, May 1955."

To Be Continued . . .

The Doll People

Ann M. Martin & Laura Godwin
Pictures by Brian Selznick